W9-BMO-602

Clayton Stone,
At Your Service

Ena Jones

Holiday House / New York

For Jeff

And for Blake, Kevin, Ena Marie and Thomas

Library of Congress Cataloging-in-Publication Data

Jones, Ena.
Clayton Stone, at your service / by Ena Jones.—First edition.
pages cm
Summary: Twelve-year-old Clayton Stone gets a taste of life as a special agent
when he goes undercover as a decoy in a high-stakes kidnapping operation.
ISBN 978-0-8234-3389-6 (hardcover)
[1. Undercover operations—Fiction.   2. Spies—Fiction.   3. Kidnapping—
Fiction.]   I. Title.
PZ7.1.J68Cl 2015
813.6—dc23
[E]
2014038323

ACKNOWLEDGMENTS

I am indebted to everyone involved in helping *Clayton Stone, At Your Service* become a book, particularly my publisher and the staff at Holiday House. I especially want to thank my editor, Sally Morgridge, who made the entire editing process a pleasure. If I lived in NYC, I'd visit her every day to give her a big, grateful hug.

I have an abundance of love and gratitude for Rebecca Barnhouse, the very best writer-friend and critique partner a person could have. She is personally responsible for my ever-deteriorating home management skills and the number of times I order pizza for dinner because she's insisted I "Keep going!"

My agent, Ginger Knowlton, the unofficial Queen of Agenting (although she would probably prefer me to say "tennis"); she has made the business side of publishing a book a calm and worry-free experience. A huge thanks to her and the staff at Curtis Brown. It's a well-oiled machine there!

I must also thank Anna Webman Silverman, previous Curtis Brown agent, who read and represented the manuscript in its infancy. Without her initial comments and urging to make the story "bigger," Clayton might never have made it past his own backyard.

I couldn't be more grateful to my fellow moderators, administrators and chief administrator, Verla, who together keep the SCBWI message board (Blueboard) running; I'm happy to call this group, and all the members of the board, my online family. Specifically, I'd like to thank Marissa Doyle, Rose Green, Evelyn Christensen, Vonna Carter and Jeff Carney, for reading and commenting on versions of the manuscript along the way.

To my very first critique group in Gainesville, Florida: Barbara Bockman, Colleen Rand, Cana Rensberger, Linda Eadie and Doug Day—years may go by, but you each remain in my heart, always.

I also want to thank my parents-in-law, Robert F. Jones, Barbara D. Jones and Richard Ashwick, for their encouragement and support of my writing over the years.

And with all the love I have, the biggest thanks to my husband, Jeff, and our children, Blake, Kevin, Ena Marie and Thomas, always willing to read a chapter, or a manuscript, but mostly I thank them for letting me turn down the music so I can hear the voices in my head.

CHAPTER ONE

The gun muzzle presses against my neck. For a second I wonder what the pavement will look like if Wacko Man pulls the trigger. A lot bloodier than any Xbox scene, no doubt.

Well, shoot. No, not shoot. I mean, dang it. How the heck did I end up in this mess?

But I know how. One stupid phone call, an overheard conversation, plus an idiot kid—me—who does exactly the opposite of what his grandmother wants, equals *this big mess*.

Thirty-six hours ago I was more boring than vanilla ice cream, doing normal seventh-grade stuff. A pretty good lacrosse player with twenty goals and half a season still ahead. Decent scores on almost every game system within a ten-mile radius. And the most average thing? I might actually pull off straight Cs this quarter at my uptight private school.

Enter Captain Thompson. Enter listening devices, disguises, GPS trackers and microphone chips. Enter me, thinking I can help save the world, or at least one mom and her daughter. There's a new definition for *sucker* on Wikipedia. It's a picture of me: Clayton Patrick Stone. And I'm not smiling.

First came the phone call.

CHAPTER TWO

I'm up in my gramps's office hanging with Bart, the stuffed buffalo, after a long, wet afternoon at lacrosse practice. The third floor was a better place to hang out when he was alive. Gramps, not Bart. I never knew Bart when he was alive.

Sometimes I can even forget that Bart's the only one to talk to up here, but then there are other times. Like right now, when I tell him the guys are coming over tomorrow and we're gonna play some video games and order burgers from Big Stone's, the diner my family owns. Gramps would have gotten real excited, maybe asked if he should run out and get the latest Madden for us. Bart just stares at me with glazed, indifferent eyes.

Gramps's office is in the attic of my grandparents' super-old stone house, with a view over the treetops. In the winter, if you stand on your tiptoes and find the exact right angle, you can see the Potomac River.

I don't do that anymore.

Anyway, after a couple of turns at Gramps's indoor putting green and a few throws at the dartboard, I slide across the wide-planked floor in my socks. I can smell Gran's pot roast, and the thought of a good dinner is making my stomach gurgle. Practice today was tough, and I am *hungry*.

Photos and awards line the long attic walls, so thick I can barely see the whitewashed plaster underneath. When I was little, Gramps used to carry me from one end of the room to the other and point out all the important people he and Gran were photographed with. "This is the secretary of state in 1982," and "This is the president of France."

I don't get why so many important people wanted a picture with the Pickle King of the world. If they only knew how much Gramps hated the pickles that made him rich!

I'm looking at a photo of Gran and Gramps with the first President Bush when a ringing phone startles me about two inches off the floor. Even though it's an office, I've never heard a phone up here before. Seriously, never.

My socks and I slide over to Gramps's desk, and I pick up the receiver. But all I get is dial tone. The phone rings again. The sound is coming from across the room...Gran's desk? If I've never heard a phone ring up here, I've twice as seriously never seen my grandmother sit at that desk. And I'd swear on a stack of Bibles she hasn't been inside this room for the last year. She won't even come up the stairs.

I fly across the room—well, not literally—and land in the chair so hard it rolls backward. I scoot forward and scan the top of the desk. I still don't see a telephone, and the high-pitched ringing seems to be getting louder. The sound is coming from somewhere inside. I tug at the top drawer. It's locked, and so is the next one. The third drawer opens and there's nothing. Until I look more closely.

In the back left corner gleams a small gold key. I grab it—could this be what I need? Only one way to—

Ha! The key turns and the top drawer opens, and there it sits: a plugged-in cell phone flashing a red strobe light and blaring long streams of noise.

Something about the ring feels wrong. My stomach forgets about the pot roast downstairs long enough to tighten, warning me to leave the phone where it is; telling me, Don't even touch it. And for sure don't answer it.

But I'm stupid that way. I bring it to my ear.

"Uh, hello?" I say.

I can hear somebody on the line, but they hesitate before they speak. When it finally comes, the voice is impatient. "Liza? He wants to speak with you. Hold on."

Since when do I sound like a sixty-year-old lady? "Uh, no. She's downstairs. Hold on a minute—I'll get her." I fumble with the cord, unplugging it from the inside of the drawer.

Sometimes I swear Gran has ESP, and this is one of those times. Because I know she's been on the first floor, cooking dinner—but just as I'm about to run and get her, there she is in the doorway, staring at me and shaking her head like something terrible has happened. But that can't be true; all the terrible things have already happened.

Then my heart stops. Behind her stands a big man in one of those serious suits, and holy mother of the Mafia, he's obviously not here to bake pies.

The man in the suit nudges Gran into the room. "Go ahead, Liza, he'll tell you everything." His tone isn't exactly friendly, but the way he says her name doesn't sound like he's here to use that not-so-concealed gun of his. So I swallow big and hold out the phone while my heart trips over itself to start pumping again.

Gran puts the phone to her ear. "This is Liza Stone."

There's a pause, and then she sighs. "Yes, sir," and "No, sir," and "But, sir, I'm not sure if...." and then, "Of course, Mr. President."

More silence, then, finally, "Yes, sir, Captain Thompson is here. I'm sure we'll figure something out. It was lovely to speak with you again, too. Good-bye, Mr. President." With a forceful poke at the screen, she hangs up the phone.

Did she say *president*?

"Gran, was that *the* president?" I point to a picture on the wall. *"Our* president?"

But Gran's not listening to me. She's glaring at the man in

the suit, her blue eyes as steely as Big Stone's kitchen. "Derek," she says. And the way her tongue slices through his name and lands hard like a guillotine on the *k*, I know she's furious. "I can't believe you've put me in this position. When Jack retired, that was the end. I have Clayton to consider."

The man in the suit—Derek—nods. "You're right. And I have Clayton to consider, too. And if Jack were alive, he'd consider Clayton. And in case you missed it, President Hampton is considering Clayton."

Each time he says my name, it feels like hot oil sizzling across my shoulders, and I know something big is going on. The president of the United States is considering me? What the heck happened, and how did my name get in the middle of this?

But Gran doesn't let him keep talking. In two strides her long, perfectly manicured fingernails are twisting around the muscular man's ear, pulling him toward the stairs like a second grader being hauled to the headmistress's office. Obviously she wants to have the rest of the conversation in private.

No way I'm gonna let that happen. I wait a couple of minutes, and then I follow them.

But I don't take the stairs.

CHAPTER THREE

There are two ways down. Big, fancy stairs in the front, and the cool way. In the rear of the house, the spiral steps are wrapped with a molded wood slide that winds its way down all three stories.

I launch myself onto the polished mahogany. All the pot-banging echoing up the stairwell as I whiz past the second floor tells me Gran's brought Serious-Suit Man to the kitchen.

I stick the landing on the first floor like a ninja and immediately drop to my knees, leaning far enough forward to spy with one eye.

Gran and "Derek" are nose to nose, Gran holding her wooden spoon in the air like a sword, and the captain's chin up and ready for it. They're going back and forth at each other in fierce whispers that carry through the doorway so well, you could easily say they're screaming—but in a battling iguanas, hissing sort of way.

"You've got the wrong boy, Derek. He's nothing like his grandfather. Or his father. I will admit, there's nobody faster on the lacrosse field. But, mercy! Yesterday I asked him to kill a spider and he practically wet his pants."

Totally unfair. It was a wolf spider the size of a tarantula. In fact, maybe it *was* a tarantula. I would have killed it if she'd handed me the bug spray. But a friggin' Kleenex pulled from her sleeve?

"Liza," says the captain, completely ignoring her. "The senator's wife and daughter were last seen shopping at Bloomingdale's thirty-six hours ago, the same location of at least four of the previous mall incidents. At the very least, we're dealing with a kidnapping—but if it turns out to be murder...You understand, the Meldons are prominent citizens. We don't have much time before the media discovers they're missing."

Gran makes a sound somewhere between a snort and a screech. "Nothing you or the president has told me indicates the Special Service should be involved. You are way outside your parameters here!"

I stare at my grandmother. She's using words like *parameters*. And *Special Service*. *What* is the Special Service? I am way confused.

She sucks in both cheeks to reel in her attitude. Usually that only happens when the dishwasher breaks at the diner and she's trying to keep her head from exploding.

Her voice gets spooky calm. "Derek, have you interviewed Senator Meldon? He needs to be thoroughly questioned about his wife and daughter's disappearance."

Silence.

"I thought not." Gran shakes her head. "Just because Carl Meldon and the president are golf buddies does not mean you can ignore standard protocol."

She's bossing the captain like she bosses me—the way she used to boss Dad, and Mom, and Gramps. I can't keep up with whatever it is she's saying—mostly because I'm still trying to figure out what *parameters* and *protocol* mean—and every time the captain tries to interrupt, she fires another machine gun's worth of words at him. "...I sit on committees with both the Meldons. And I admire Mary Lou. She comes from the Lennox family, but you wouldn't know it, and she devotes a good deal of her time and money to extremely important causes."

"Exactly why we need to find them. She makes even more things happen around this town than her husband. If the mall napper—"

Gran doesn't let him finish. "Derek, I understand you think this may be related to the mall napper crimes, but regardless of the Meldons' political stature, that is no reason for you to show up at this house practically demanding to use my grandson as bait..." Her voice gets sharper with each word and finally lowers again as she accuses him with a glassy, hard stare. "You know we've already lost Jack and Clayton's parents in service to this country. Don't you think the Stones have given enough?"

Okay. Now that they're talking about me and my family, my brain starts processing faster than a Formula One in the heat of a race—but it's not sure which lane to take. Gramps served the country? Like my parents? But he wasn't in the navy. Or army. Or anything. And they want to use *me* as "bait"? To get the mall napper dude?

The mall napper is the reason some parents have been bordering on the paranoid side of overprotective. We live in Virginia, right across the river from Washington, DC. For almost a month, some bozo has been capturing moms with their kids and making the moms drive to an ATM to get cash.

Half the time he screws up somehow and ends up getting away with nothing—or not as much as he wants, at least. The biggest problem is his gun. "Nothing worse than an idiot with a gun," says Gran. The police want to catch him before somebody gets hurt.

But if this is the same person, and he's starting to seriously kidnap—or murder—there might be a reason to stay home and lock the doors.

I stand up and walk into the kitchen.

Gran is saying something about "appropriate channels," and I see the captain inflate his chest and grow six inches closer to the ceiling. His voice sounds like rumbling thunder as it bellows over her; this time he has her attention.

"Liza, you know the Special Service does undercover better than any agency around, but we don't have a kid. And to pull this off we need one. *Today!* We wouldn't ask if this weren't a critical situation. And that's the reason we thought of Clayton; yes, he's athletic, but most of all, he's got Stone blood. Whether you think so or not, he takes after—" He abruptly stops when he notices I'm standing beside him, but I know he was about to say my grandfather's name.

Gran looks at me, and then back at the captain, and for a fraction of a second I see her eyes glisten. I don't know how this man knows us, but Gramps was involved with him somehow. And that's got to be why Gran's upset. Is she remembering the three days Gramps was missing? Before they found his body on the banks of the Potomac? As fast as it came, the moment is gone; her eyes are dry and solid Stone again.

My grandmother steps over and wraps her arm around my shoulders. "Clayton, Captain Thompson was about to leave."

They need a kid, and the president himself sent the captain here. I stare up at Captain Thompson, and the words somehow stumble out of my mouth. "Maybe I should try to help, Gran."

The captain clamps down on his lower lip and raises his eyebrows, sending my grandmother a wordless question. After a few seconds, she lets out a sigh and sets her wooden spoon on the counter. She moves to the kitchen table and reluctantly nods at us as she takes a seat. "Well?" she says.

The corner of the captain's mouth curls victoriously, and he turns and sits beside her, pushing a chair out for me to join them.

I do. Captain Thompson looks at Gran for a moment and then stares directly into my eyes. "Why don't I tell you about our plan?"

CHAPTER FOUR

Less than twenty-four hours later, I'm in the underwear section at Macy's. Shopping. Normally, I wouldn't be caught dead here. Now I might be.

Caught dead, that is.

I lean over and mutter to my shoe, trying to act like bra-shopping with my fake mom is a regular day in the life of me. "Can you hear me? Over."

By order of Gran, I've been plastered with every possible listening device and GPS tracker. Microphone chips are sewn into my collar, embedded in my watch and superglued to my belt buckle. Can they hear me? Holy mother of micromanagement, of course they can hear me.

A gruff voice hits my ear and I can practically see the captain's forehead do that back-and-forth accordion squeeze, like cars on the Beltway at rush hour. "Clayton, don't talk back to me, or anyone. How many times do I have to tell you? There's going to be all sorts of communication over this frequency. Don't speak to anyone but Agent Moxie—and remember, she *is* supposed to be your mom."

I adjust the iPod wire hanging from my ear. "Got it."

"Clayton, I mean it. Not another word."

"I said okay!" What does he expect when he gets me up at 6 a.m. for three hours of training? It's taken two ginormous Cokes to keep my eyes open. Does the man think I'm gonna do everything right?

Between rainstorms, we've made three trips to the SUV in three different lots, all from different stores, at different malls. So far, no bad guy. This time we parked it way deep in the Macy's parking garage. And the sun's finally come out.

Agent Moxie—my fake mom—puts her hand on her hip and glares at me from across the rack of black doodads she's whizzing through. She points to a spot a few feet away. "Billy, why don't you sit beside the cash register while I look at these nightgowns?" Her polite tone doesn't match the flamethrower look in her eyes. No doubt, she's slick. Not even the saleslady has caught a whiff of her disagreeable personality.

And when did she decide to call me Billy? *Billy?* Huge note to self: next time—if there is a next time—I pick my own code name.

I sit in the chair and start messing with the half-rigged iPod some technician wearing glasses and a lab coat gave me during my "emergency training" session. Actually, he called it a SpiPod, and then chuckled, like that was funny. What does he think this is, an Alex Rider adventure?

"Okay, we're almost set," says Captain Thompson, his voice penetrating the earbuds. "Clayton, you follow Agent Moxie's lead. Same as before, you'll approach the vehicle like a regular mom and kid. You know what I mean, Clayton. Pay more attention to your iPod than to the fact that you're walking through a parking garage. Click the Forward button if you understand."

It's way tempting to say something, but I keep my mouth shut and tap the screen with my thumb.

"Great. And remember the sedative stick we gave you. Just in case. It'll put him out immediately if things go haywire. Okay?"

I tap the screen again, wishing there were an Eye Roll button.

"Good," says Captain Thompson. He pauses, then murmurs

something I can't decipher. After another few seconds, he continues his brief. "Now, Moxie, we've got one guy hanging out by the entrance. He's a definite watch. There's another pacing up and down the ramp, talking on a cell. He might be moving because he keeps losing reception, or he could be waiting for his wife—who knows? We'll probably do this a few more times today, because neither one of these guys matches our target's profile."

After a brief pause, the captain says, "Let's try this again—thirty seconds. Remember, all you need to do is draw this guy out of hiding. Once we're sure it's him, our people will move in."

I stare at Agent Moxie as she checks something in her over-sized purse. She's dressed in a canary-yellow jogging suit that definitely cost some bucks, and she looks exactly like all the rich ladies who shop at the Galleria. She puts her cell to her ear and finishes listening to the captain.

"Come on, Billy, we've got to get going." Agent Moxie's command is all the warning I get—the canary is in flight, heading for the department store exit. I stick the other bud in my ear and rush to catch up.

We move through the electronic doors, and I try to keep my eyes fixed on the screen of my SpiPod. Twice I look up, hoping to spot the guys the agents are watching, but the captain is on me. "Clayton, pay attention to what you're supposed to be doing!"

Oh. My. God. But I do my best to cross the street and walk toward the mall parking garage like a normal kid. Only, that's sort of impossible. I'm carrying an instant-deep-sleep sedative stick in the pocket of sagging black jeans that Gran would *never* let me wear in real life. And then there's Mr. Big Shot shouting in my ear. *Nothing* about this day is ordinary.

As we enter the garage, shafts of afternoon sun beam between the massive concrete columns, but any real light is fading fast, and the farther we walk, the creepier it feels. Even squinting, I can barely see the silver SUV we're headed toward. I shuffle along, struggling to keep up with the super-stride of Agent Moxie.

"Moxie? Clayton? I'm getting static. Can you hear me? Hold up!" It's the captain's voice, and he sounds uptight.

I raise my eyes to my "mother." Can't she hear the captain yelling at us? Is she ignoring him? Crud. What the heck am I supposed to do?

I slow my pace. "Hey, Mom."

She turns. "Yes, Billy?"

I hold out one of my earbuds. "Listen to this song."

"Billy, we need to get home."

Jeez. She *is* slick. That's exactly what a real mom would say.

"C'mon, Mom, you'll like it." If the captain wants us to hold up, there has to be a darn good reason. This guy we're after has struck almost every day for the last few weeks. Now that he's maybe kidnapped the senator's wife and daughter, Captain Thompson says he's getting greedy, and that makes him even more dangerous.

Agent Moxie gives her head an impatient shake and snaps the tiny piece of plastic out of my hand, stretching the cord. It's not long enough, so she gives it another good yank and holds it to her ear.

My other earbud is now hanging down my shirt, and I tighten my grip on the SpiPod. I cock an eyebrow at her and whisper, "Something must be wrong with your earpiece."

She purses her lips and nods. Only, it's not nodding. She's trying to move her head to the beat of the band she's not listening to. Huh. There's a lot to this undercover stuff.

Agent Moxie finally takes out the earpiece and, with a weird smile, gives it back to me. In a loud voice she says, "That wasn't bad." Then she puts her arm around me and begins to move toward the SUV. She squeezes my shoulder and whispers, "You were right. Apparently, my earpiece *isn't* working. The captain says there's a man headed this way, but he's pretty far behind us. They've backed off surveillance to give him room. Stay on the driver's side of the truck so we aren't separated."

I feel the blood pulsing through my neck as Agent Moxie

pulls away from me. She's still got that disturbing smile on her face as we approach the vehicle, and it occurs to me: Does she have a gun? More important, is she ready to use it?

Man, what was I thinking? That this was going to be cool? My birthday is on Friday. Carlos from the diner said he'd make my favorite cake, the one stuffed with custard and fresh strawberries. I've been looking forward to eating it since January. Now I just want to *make* it to Friday.

We're ten steps away. The truck has tinted windows and we can't see inside. And we can't see through to the other side where somebody might be standing. Waiting.

Fear and regret are pumping through my bloodstream and my legs are floating forward, like all gravity has disappeared.

Five steps away. I scan the other cars parked sporadically around us and tell myself we'll be okay. All we have to do is get this guy.

Agent Moxie pushes the remote button on her key chain. The doors of the SUV click and the lights flash hello.

Three more steps. Nobody around. Maybe we got this all wrong. Agent Moxie walked too fast. Maybe we'll go to another store and try all over again. And this time I'll duck into the bathroom and hide until dinner.

Two steps. Agent Moxie reaches for the door handle as my shoes crunch something. She turns at the sound and her eyes flit past me; she opens her mouth as the captain speaks in my ear.

"Clayton, tell Agent Mo—" That's all I get before a dark force comes from behind and wraps a monster arm across my body. Then, as if the message isn't clear enough, he squeezes my rib cage and bends my arm so hard I squeak. I can't move, and I don't know whether it's from fear or it's physically impossible, but I can't make another sound, either.

The earbuds drop from my ears, one at a time, and dangle for a split second before landing with the SpiPod on the concrete below.

Agent Moxie ricochets off the SUV, ready to fight, but the

monster of a man puts something hard against my neck. It hurts. And by the look on Agent Moxie's face, I know it could hurt a lot more.

"You turn around and get in," the man snarls at Agent Moxie. "We're going for a ride."

He pushes me against the SUV. "You, too, rugrat."

I lock eyes with my fake mom. I guess we'll listen. At least for the next minute or so.

CHAPTER FIVE

Okay, so I should have realized guns and bad guys are much worse than even the biggest spiders. This is crazy. Wacko Man can pull the trigger right now and *I will die.*

Agent Moxie is staring at us, but I'm afraid to move. The guy squeezes me again and presses my body against the SUV, my face squashed goldfish-style against the pitch-black window. I'm pretty much wondering where Captain Thompson's people are. Um, hello? Underage and totally innocent kid to captain: Do you see what's going on here?

I watch Agent Moxie's eyes travel from the man's face to his shoes, probably memorizing every detail.

"Please don't hurt my son," she says, her voice shaking. "You can put the gun away. I'll do anything you want. I beg you, don't hurt him."

"Lady, just get in and drive to an ATM," says Wacko Man. "Do what I say and the kid stays quiet, there'll be no problem. All I want is my payday."

Agent Moxie's hands are, I hope, fake-trembling as she jabs the jumble of keys in the air, frantically aiming the remote at the SUV. The car doors start clicking and clacking while the lights flash and the horn beeps, and she's babbling in a high-pitched voice, "Billy, it's going to be okay," over and over.

She's obviously stalling, and making noise. Something Wacko Man Does. Not. Like. *"Lady!* What are you doing? Open the #$@&% door!" He charges toward Agent Moxie and grabs at the keys, pulling me with him.

I squirm and try to maneuver out of his grasp as he rushes her, without snapping something essential, like my neck. But he just drags me with him, squeezing even tighter than before. My head is forced downward, and I notice peanut shells. There's actually a whole one that hasn't been cracked—*Sheesh,* Clayton. *Focus!*

Agent Moxie is telling the man to calm down so she can unlock the car, lifting the keys farther out of reach. And since he's got ahold of me, he can't get to them.

"Lady, get in the car. *Now!"* He sounds like a dad arguing with a two-year-old who won't listen. And then he farts. Loud.

I snort; yes, there's a gun on me, but I can't help it. The guy turns on me. "What's so funny, brat?"

Do I really have to explain?

Out of the corner of my eye, I see Agent Moxie back up and look around the parking garage. What's she trying to do?

Duh. She can't do anything while this guy has a gun on me. Nobody can. And even though the captain is watching, and listening, too, everybody's in a holding pattern, because no agent in their right mind can approach us. That's just Bad Guy Holding a Kid at Gunpoint 101.

Wacko Man reaches for the driver's door handle and pulls with his free hand. The door doesn't open, and he whines like a kid. "Gimme those keys!" he says, lunging at Agent Moxie.

This guy's brain waves are measuring at the lower end of the Richter scale of intelligence, and if he keeps jerking me around like this, the gun thrust against my jugular is going to go off by accident.

Agent Moxie backs up again, starting to look a little nervous for real. "I'll open it, just please don't hurt my son."

He hesitates for a second, then yanks me back to the rear passenger door and puts his free hand on the handle, waiting for her to unlock the SUV.

I gotta get away from him. Doesn't matter that Agent Moxie is right here with me. Doesn't matter that there are thirty special agents within a two-block radius. Doesn't matter about the sedative stick in my pocket—

Or maybe it does.

I look between Agent Moxie and Wacko Man, who are locked in a stare-down as she fumbles like a huge klutz with the remote, and I finger the hard ridge of the sedative stick in my pocket. The captain says the microneedle is the lab's latest invention: a tenth as wide as a human hair, exactly like silk—and dagger-strong. The guy won't even feel it. And I did practice using it—on a banana.

Like it or not, it's our only way out.

Moving in triple-slow motion, I slip the stick out of my pocket and, holding it in my palm, slide the cap off, like the captain showed me. I pray Wacko Man will keep his eyes on Agent Moxie, but just as I'm going to make my move, he lets go of me and lurches for her; pointing the gun with a long groan, he shakes his head. "Oh, hell, lady, just give me your purse!"

Agent Moxie's eyes flash wide with surprise; now she's the one with a gun on her.

Finally free, I see my chance. Holding tight to the plastic vial, I propel myself on top of Wacko Man, knocking his gun into the air. We both topple over, and I swing my hand around, aiming the nuclear-strong microneedle at him. As we fall, I somehow get blocked by Agent Moxie's legs and bring her to the ground with us.

The longest-ever two and a half seconds later, a dozen agents surround the three of us, tangled on top of each other on the concrete. Relief comes breathing out of me as one of them kicks Wacko Man's gun down the pavement.

Then I hear somebody snicker.

I don't get it. Until I see my hand, still clutching the sedative stick, which is stuck hard and deep into Agent Moxie's canary-yellow jogging suit. Her mouth falls open and she lets out a loud snore.

"Wrong leg, dude," says a voice from above. And the rest of the suits start to laugh.

CHAPTER SIX

I follow Captain Thompson out of his black Suburban into a brick office building. We zigzag down three different hallways and turn left into a medium-sized office, where he shuts the door behind us. He's been on his cell phone since we stepped inside the Suburban, but I have no idea what's happening, because all he's done is grunt.

I'm guessing this is his office. It's pretty bare, though. No art, no photographs; even the walls are a dull gray. On the left side of the desk is a putting green. He points to a chair and we both sit while he finishes his call.

When he finally hangs up, he tucks his phone inside his blazer. Then, from out of nowhere, my cell phone appears on the desk. "I need the iPod, Clayton."

I put the now-broken SpiPod on the desk and pick up my cell. I push at the side, but it's no use; the thing is dead and buried and will take forever to charge. Crud. I should have turned it off before handing it over. Not that I get why he took it in the first place.

As if he can read my mind, the captain shakes his finger at me. "Can't ever risk an agent's distraction, Clayton, and personal cell phones are the worst."

I slide my phone into my jeans pocket. "Aren't you going to debrief me?"

"No, Clayton. I was there, remember? I saw everything. Right now we're just waiting for your grandmother."

Is his personality set to permanent grouch?

"Yeah, well, I Googled spy stuff last night. It seems like that's what should happen next." I want him to know I take this job seriously.

"Normally it is, but this is a special case. So let's just take it one step at a time."

I almost get through promising myself I'm not going to ask another question, when a big one pops into my head. "So, did Agent Moxie wake up?"

Captain Thompson cocks his head and sort of smiles to himself. "She's awake, yes," he says. "But she's more than a little cranky."

Yeah, she probably hates me big-time now. Not that she liked me much to begin with. "So am I in trouble?"

"Trouble." He says it as a statement. "Real trouble is when one of the good guys dies. Today, a few things could have gone better, but in the end, we got the suspect, and that's what counts."

He stands up and gestures out the darkened window behind him. "We couldn't have taken him like that if it hadn't been for you, Clayton. Despite what happened with Agent Moxie, you were the one who turned the game around. I'm pretty impressed."

A thrill runs through my body. The guy we got has been all over the news for weeks. And even though I screwed up with the sedative stick, the captain is impressed.

Clearing his throat, he continues. "I know we've discussed this, but I need to be sure you understand, your involvement in this case is top secret. You can't discuss it—not one bit of it—with anyone. No friends, no trusted teachers, no girlfriends. Is that clear?"

Girlfriends? Is he kidding?

His eyes, creased and intense, bore into me, and his lips

are pressed tight. He's waiting for my response. I'm afraid he's gonna pull out a Bible and make me swear on Gran's life or something. I sit up straight and look him in the eye. "Yes, sir."

"Good."

With another click of the pen, his shoulders relax and he moves on to real business. "The suspect's name is Wheeler— Bob Wheeler. And he's developed a serious case of lockjaw; but if there's a link between him and the senator's wife and daughter, we'll figure it out."

Shoot. For a second I thought it was all over. I almost forgot about the senator's family. "You think you'll get him to talk?"

The captain shrugs, walks over to the door and opens it. "Once he realizes that's the only way he can help himself—probably." He pokes his head into the hallway and looks both ways.

It occurs to me, since he's waiting for Gran, that I should warn him. "Uh, Captain, we might not want to tell her the Wheeler guy had a gun to my neck. I think she'd go a little nuts if she found out."

"I am acutely aware of what it takes to deal with your grandmother, Clayton."

That's what he thinks. "I'm just saying. She might be old, but she runs a diner and she gets major mad when somebody tries to pull something on her—like stealing meat, or stuff like that."

The captain raises his chin thoughtfully and ambles over to the corner of the office. He picks up a golf club leaning against the wall, then pulls a white ball out of his pocket and sets it on the green. "Yes, you're right. But we're not trying to pull anything on her." Facing me, he pauses to square his body and adjust his grip. He gently strokes the ball and we both watch it roll down the green, straight into the hole.

The captain retrieves it and returns to the top of the green. "The fact is, Clayton, we were all acting in the line of duty. Me, Agent Moxie, the other agents—and you. Sometimes that means putting it all on the line and taking chances. We may need to remind your grandmother of that."

Duty. I've heard that word a lot over the past almost thirteen years. There was one time—one specific time—that I don't want to think about. I try to replace the memory with something else. Ice cream. Scoring a goal. Jumping on a trampoline.

But it's too late. 'Cause even though it happened two years ago, I can see it like it's right here, in full color. I can almost touch them. My mom and dad, sitting on our family room couch, telling me they're going to the Middle East on a special assignment for the navy and that Gran and Gramps will be taking care of me.

My dad is reaching out, putting his hand on my shoulder, saying, "Son, it's our duty. Not many people know the Arabic language and culture the way your mother and I do. We'll be helping the peace effort by translating and working on documents and—" Then he just stops talking.

I'll never understand why he didn't finish that sentence. He and Mom just hugged each other, and me.

I swallow the ache that comes from missing my parents. Because if I keep going, I know there's an ache that's even worse, and I don't want to go there; it's when I wonder how, exactly, they died. I keep staring hard. Really, really hard. The golf club, still in the captain's hands, comes into focus. I lift my eyes to meet his.

"Are you okay, Clayton?" he says.

I nod, not yet trusting myself to speak.

As if he knows I need a minute to get control, he spins the club and offers it to me. "Your turn."

I take the golf club, and as soon as I do, begin to feel steadier. I start to move in, to take the captain's place, and quickly realize that won't work. So I turn back around and face him, across the green.

The captain gives me a strange look, and I think I know why. "Yeah, I'm left-handed, just like Gramps."

"I never realized that," he says.

I take my time before I hit the ball, and the moment I send it to the hole, another vision appears in my mind. Only this time, instead of from two years ago, this one is from a few short hours ago. "You know, it's weird. That Bob Wheeler? He's left-handed, too."

Captain Thompson reaches out and puts his hand on my shoulder. "Are you sure?"

Am I sure? I carefully replay the image of Wheeler, remembering how he held me, and how he brandished his gun at Agent Moxie.

"Yeah. I'm sure. Gramps taught me to notice stuff like that. He said in an attack you gotta pay attention so you can figure how somebody's gonna come at you. I always thought he was talking about lacrosse. Now I'm thinking—" I hesitate, taking a deep breath. Maybe now's the time to push my luck. I want to know for sure. "You keep saying stuff about my grandfather. He worked—here. With you?"

A funny expression comes over Captain Thompson's face and he nods, but before the actual "Yes" can come out of his mouth, Gran rushes through the doorway.

She looks me up and down and grabs both my shoulders. "You're all right? He didn't hurt you?"

"I'm good. Captain Thompson has been very nice," I say with a straight face.

"Ha!" It's a screech, not a laugh, and before I can object, her arms are wrapped tight around me. "I didn't think this through. I thought Captain Thompson would be ready to deal with that man if he got too close to you."

She lets go, finally, and turns to Captain Thompson. They lock eyes and there's a hair's worth of absolute silence—about as much warning as anybody gets from Gran—before she digs her nails into the sleeve of his perfectly pressed black suit and drags him out of the office, swinging the door behind them. Another one of her "private" conversations.

But there's nothing private about it, because I'm two steps behind and manage to catch the door with my foot. My ear is pressed through the crack, into the hallway, and I hear every syllable of Gran's quick-tempo lecture.

"Derek, what the devil were you thinking? Moxie is furious, and I don't blame her. Clayton's nowhere near ready to deal with this kind of operation. There are years of training involved before *anyone* is ready."

"Liza, he's a smart, quick-thinking young man. We had everything under control, and even when—"

Gran cuts him off. "It was a bumbling mess, and there's no excuse for it! The entire thing should have ended before they got near the vehicle. Where was your sharpshooter?"

I can tell the captain is trying to be calm, but now his defenses, and his tone, are heading north. "There was virtually no risk to Clayton. And he came out of this like a true Stone; he's practically got *Civic Duty* engraved on his heart."

"*Virtually* no risk? You and I know what that really means."

I'm kind of liking this. It's like a parent-teacher conference on steroids, and for once the teacher's on my side.

"He's too young, Derek. My first priority is to bring that boy up. And he needs to *live* for that to happen."

The click-clack of her heels echoes down the hallway, and I know she's heading in my direction—fast. I back into the office and lean against the wall.

They both blow into the room like they've been caught in a hurricane-force wind, and Gran's jaw is clenched tight. Pit bull tight.

The captain looks shell-shocked, but I did warn him. You've gotta be on your game to win against Gran. Only, I think she's forgetting one simple fact: she's the boss at the diner, not here.

Gran takes my arm, and as she pulls me out of the office, I turn to say good-bye to Captain Thompson. But before I can open my mouth, he cocks his head and sends me a half-smile—and then he salutes.

And that's when I know the argument isn't over.

CHAPTER SEVEN

Monday morning, my best friend, Toby, is a no-show in the atrium of Masters Academy. Which is just wrong, because we always meet here and he always brings mochas from his dad's coffee shop. I stand in the middle of increasing chaos as kids rush past me in their blue blazers and ties to get to homeroom. But it's nothing compared to the chaos inside my head.

My brain hasn't stopped brewing since yesterday. With a simple nod, Captain Thompson told me: Gramps was an agent. Then there's my phone. Once it charged, there were practically a million texts from the guys on the lacrosse team. I didn't read them and can only imagine what they said. I'd invited the guys over for lunch and video games yesterday, and when everything with Captain Thompson moved so fast, I completely forgot to cancel. Who knows how long they waited?

And now I'm wondering, is that why Toby is MIA? I get it, sort of, but would he be so mad that he wouldn't show this morning?

I wait until final bell and then sprint to homeroom, taking the only desk left near the rear of the class. I turn in my seat, to Dion, and he stares back at me—practically through me.

"Where were you yesterday? Coach ran us hard because you didn't show." He stands and walks up the aisle with a shake-off attitude, like he can't get far enough away.

And then the whole unfortunate picture flashes like a huge neon *Duh!* Coach must have called a Sunday practice because of the big games this week. Crud. Crud. Crud.

I didn't show, first at my house, and then on the field, and Coach made them run. And from the look on Dion's face, and the way Toby stood me up this morning, they probably had to do suicides. Like, forever.

The entire team must hate me.

The day doesn't get any better. Not one guy on the team is saying a word to me. I sit with them at lunch—but only long enough to stuff a piece of pizza down my throat. It doesn't feel good going down, that's for sure.

When I make it to practice, the locker room is already empty, so I get into my gear and jog to the field. Coach is talking with one of the guys as I pass, but he doesn't say a word—doesn't even look up.

After a few stretches, Coach leads a series of offensive drills, and by the third rotation, I'm getting the message that this isn't going to blow over; the ball is either slamming me or it's way out of reach. Coach calls a scrimmage, and the rotten feeling that's been growing in my stomach since lunch threatens to erupt. The guys are seriously mad.

But I can't even explain, because even though I trust them on the field, or with anything at all—I don't want to know what Captain Thompson does to somebody who blabs.

We divide into four groups for two separate scrimmages, six on six, on each half of the field. Toby and I are on Field A, but on opposite teams.

My team ignores me, play after play. It takes forever before I finally manage to snatch the ball from the air. And then I feel a shadow on me, coming hard and fast. It's Toby, with both hands on his stick and a fire in his eyes like I've never seen. I know I can't avoid what I've got coming. When he hits me, I go flying, and the next thing I know, I'm on the ground and he's walking away and all I can hope is that he feels better, because I sure don't.

Real secrets suck.

CHAPTER EIGHT

Two hours later, it's no better at home, but for a different reason. From the second I walk into the kitchen, I can tell Gran's mood is the same as last night.

"Clayton Patrick Stone, you sit down and do your homework," she says, tears flowing down her cheeks. She's ignoring them, though. She just keeps chopping. "See how upset you're making me? Why do I have to remind you about your homework? You're in seventh grade—practically grown."

I roll my eyes. "Gran, stop it. You're not upset. It's the onions."

Gran scowls and shakes her head, and her knife, at me. "A boy as smart as you shouldn't get Cs, much less Ds, on his report card. And don't tell me I'm not upset. I *am* upset. I'm downright crazy with upsetness."

I sit at the kitchen table and pull my history textbook from my backpack. I open it to chapter nine and try to disappear between the pages. We're studying the Civil War, but I'm not sure why. History is a pointless subject. Once people are dead, it's over. If there were a class called Future, maybe there'd be a reason to pay attention.

I feel Gran hovering. I don't want to, but I look up.

"Just so we're clear, this is the end of the road. If you'll remember, your birthday is Friday. It will be very nice if you reach the age of thirteen with all your body parts intact. I told Derek there will be no more 'assignments' for you."

"They want me for more assignments?"

No answer. Okay, time for another tactic. "You seem to know him really well."

She purses her lips and says a very quick "No." Then she takes a breath and lets it out. "Yes," she says, briefly shutting her eyes. When she opens them, she stares at me for a few seconds, then walks back to the counter, picks up her knife and points it at me. "Forget I said anything. Trust me, and forget *everything*."

Maybe I should keep my mouth shut, but I can't stop myself. "I *know*, Gran. I know all about Gramps being an agent."

She takes a deep breath before she responds. "Clayton, you may think you've learned all there is to know about your grandfather, but you have no idea. And you especially don't know what danger is."

Is she kidding? *I* don't know what danger is? I'm the one who had a gun pressed against my neck yesterday. But before I can argue, she goes on. "It's time I explained why I am so concerned. This is not only about your grandfather. It's about your parents, too."

"Yeah, I get it. They were in the navy, and—"

She holds her hand up to stop me. "Yes, Clayton. They met at the Naval Academy and received much of their training there. And generally, only people with top-level security clearance know this, but several years after your parents graduated, the Special Service recruited them to work undercover, just like your grandfather."

"They weren't—translators?"

"Not in the usual sense. They didn't sit behind desks and translate documents and wiretaps, no."

"What, then?"

"Clayton, your parents became highly specialized agents. It's impossible for me to disclose everything, but as you're aware, they were both fluent in several dialects of Arabic. As a result, they were assigned to work a very important undercover operation in the Middle East."

Gran is silent for a minute, letting me take in her words.

"So that's why they were killed. Somebody bad found out?"

Gran nods. "It wasn't just a tragedy for our family when we lost your parents. It was a tragedy for the people of the Middle East, and even the world."

She takes a deep breath before continuing. "This is why I am concerned about your involvement with the Special Service. There is a sense of duty required in this business—and you, Clayton, are not an adult. It's practically impossible for you to understand what you are risking."

Risk. Duty. Two words I've heard my whole life. It's as if my parents and grandfather are standing here with us. Their lives are starting to make sense. And now, so is mine.

"You're right; maybe I don't understand. But I helped put that man in jail yesterday. Me. I helped. A lot. For the first time in forever, I won at something that wasn't related to sports or Xbox. Doesn't that count for something?"

"Clayton, this isn't a game." But her cheeks fall and the expression on her face changes. I have to keep going.

"I know it's not a game, Gran. And I know you promised Mom and Dad you'd take care of me. But I could get knocked out playing lacrosse, or football. I could get hit by a car. Anytime. Anywhere. Mom and Dad always talked about 'duty,' even when they were scared. And remember what Gramps used to say?"

Her eyes begin to fill. "Don't."

I let out the breath I've been holding. *"Risk is everywhere."*

Gran lays the knife on the cutting board and grips the kitchen counter. I know this might be my only opportunity to reach her. "So I took a risk, Gran, and who knows how many people it helped? I could score a hundred goals, or get a thousand As, but nothing would make me feel like I did yesterday. I did a good job, and—"

Two non-onion tears stream down her face. "And?"

I get up from my seat and hug her. "Gran?" I step back. "You know how our country needed Mom and Dad—and Gramps?"

She squeezes her eyes shut as if she already knows what I'm about to say.

I hold tight to her arms. "What if it needs me, too?"

After homework and the quietest dinner ever, I head to my room. I flop on my bed and glance reluctantly at my phone. I should text Toby, but this whole thing is beyond a "Sorry." They think I skipped out on them yesterday, and missing practice was like nailing my coffin shut with iron spikes.

We've got a tough game Wednesday against St. Ignatius. And if Toby and I can't get this thing turned around, forget it.

I pick up my cell and start to read some of the texts I missed yesterday. I cringe as I scroll. One right after the other:

Where r u?
Man, it's raining. Get out of bed.
R u kidding?
C'mon. We're starving.
4get u C
Watch ur back @ practice

And then they get bad. I sink into my pillow, putting the whole picture together. They thought I was sleeping. Ignoring them. Then they probably thought I ditched practice Sunday because they were mad about waiting in the rain.

No benefit of the doubt, or anything! These guys are supposed to be my friends. I've never said I'd be somewhere and not shown up. Never. What if I'd been sick in a hospital bed or something? Heck, they could have at least asked what happened.

I stop and think about that, realizing I would have had to

lie. That I am lying. And that I will have to lie again to keep the secret.

Forget it. This whole thing has got to get straight, and the only way to make that happen is to—talk.

"I shouldn't even answer, y'know," Toby says after five long rings.

"Listen, Toby, I'm really sorry. I had to do something with Gran yesterday—one of her friends came into town and I forgot to call you. Gran made me leave my cell at home." It might be a tiny speck of the truth, but I know I'm not the only kid who gets his phone confiscated when his parents want his full attention. As I wait for Toby to respond, I scramble for something Gran and I could have done all day.

Toby groans. "Well, I hope you had a good time with the geriatric crowd. Do you know what happened? We ended up at my house—but my dad came home and kicked everybody out. And when you didn't show for practice, Coach asked where you were. And somebody said you were probably still sleeping, and Coach didn't think that was funny. He started with a hundred push-ups. Then suicides. And then he made us run the track until even Runner looked like he was ready to puke. But he had nothing to puke up, 'cause we were all supposed to eat at your house."

Now I'm wondering if Coach's silent treatment means he's gonna bench me Wednesday. He's always said he'd rather lose than play somebody who isn't a hundred percent committed to the team.

"I'm really sorry. There wasn't anything I could do. I couldn't even check the website to see if practice was on."

Toby lets out a big sigh. I can tell he's still borderline. "You couldn't? Where the heck were you?"

It's killing me not to spill *everything*. "You wouldn't believe me if I told you." And that's all I can think of to say. I wait for the silence to end, and finally, it does.

"If you weren't my best friend, I'd have killed you, or I would have at least let everybody else at you."

"Yeah? You mean you were goin' easy on me at practice today?"

"Something like that."

That's as close to off the hook as I'm gonna get, and I'll take it.

"See you in the morning?" I say.

"Sure," says Toby. And then the line goes dead.

So we might put the team back together by Wednesday, but now the question is, will I be playing?

CHAPTER NINE

Every morning Gramps would leave my tie hanging on my door-knob before school. But after he died, Gran said I'd have to figure that "boy" stuff out on my own. Her only explanation: "A young man should know how to dress himself." Really I think it was because she had no idea how to tie a tie, but thanks to the Internet, I solved the problem, and I now know three different knots for the noose I wear to school.

I get downstairs sporting the "Prince Albert" and have barely enough time to down a bagel and grab my backpack before we're out the door and in the car with Gran reciting the list of things she has to do today. We pull up to Masters and she finishes her ten-minute sentence, "...so I might be a few minutes late picking you up from practice," and hands me a banana. It's supposed to balance out the sausage pizza I have for lunch every day.

I get my gear and start up the school steps, combing my way through bunches of kids huddled together. After a series of waves, nods and "what's ups," I make it inside the front hall, where Toby's waiting with two mochas from Coffee Clutch. At least one thing's back to normal.

I drop my lacrosse bag and backpack, stick my banana inside one of the pockets and taste my mocha.

"Thanks, man," I say after the first swallow.

"No prob," he answers, absent the big Toby grin. I guess we're not completely back to normal, but he's here and that's a start.

The morning goes by okay. A lot better than yesterday, anyway. The history quiz isn't that bad, except for the names of the generals I can't keep straight, so I'm feeling pretty good as I walk into the cafeteria for lunch. The guys are all clumped around our usual tables, and even though the chatter stops as I walk up, when Toby moves over to make room for me, the mood relaxes enough for me to at least take a few bites of pizza.

Gramps would tell me to face it head-on.

It's now or never. I stare back at, like, twenty faces, and take a deep breath. "Listen, guys. About Sunday—I'm sorry. A friend of my grandmother's came to town and I sorta got . . . kidnapped for the day. I swear I'll make it up to you."

I get a few nods, and Percy elbows me. "We count on you, Clayton, and for you not to show, it—"

I nod back at all of them. "I know. It was a total jerk move. But can we please start thinking about St. Ignatius instead? 'Cause we gotta kick some butt tomorrow!"

And that's when the attitude stops and the game talk begins. Toby's laughing and the guys are claiming goals and hits and making plans to settle the score against the team that beat us less than seven days ago. It's all good.

And then Laci Peters walks up to our table, and lunch is ruined.

If there ever was an opposite of me, it's her. She's like freaky smart. Everybody expects her to be the CEO of Apple, or the president of Coke, or something insignificant like that. Even her birthday parties (which my mom used to make me go to) are run like board meetings with agendas. Twenty minutes for whatever game she's picked. A minute and a half to sing "Happy

Birthday." Five minutes to scarf down the daintiest piece of cake you've ever seen, and thirty seconds to say good-bye and thanks.

The best year was when Laci chose whacking a piñata for the game. I've always been pretty good with a stick, but adding a blindfold and lots of spinning throws off a guy's aim. Or maybe it doesn't. 'Cause I whacked Laci's ear pretty good.

After that, my mom said I didn't have to go to Laci's parties— not that I was invited anymore.

The thing is, like her birthday parties, Laci thinks Masters is a business, and she's the boss. So she prances around here with a fake smile plastered on her face, making everybody do what she wants. Yes, *prances*. Some people might call it good posture, but I think it looks like she's got a stick up her . . . well, okay, I won't go there.

So the queen is here, leaning against our table. I know she wants something. She wouldn't be here if she didn't. She's got all the guys' attention, and Toby is the worst. He gets halfway to his feet and flashes a totally dork grin. "Hey, Laci! What's up?"

I look away, hoping to avoid whatever job she's out to fill. Last time it was washing dishes for the teachers' luncheon. I get ready to slide off the bench and escape from the table.

"I promised to bring pretzels for the student council breakfast on Thursday—Headmistress Templeton always brings her homemade bran muffins that she makes with no butter, no sugar and no salt. We can't eat them again. So I told her I'd take care of everything—but I just found out Pretzel Power is closed. For good."

"What about donuts?" suggests Toby.

Laci shakes her head. "We made such a big deal about the pretzels, and told Headmistress Templeton she *had* to taste them. If I don't bring them and get donuts instead, well, it might hurt her feelings. She might see that we don't want her muffins."

This is so stupid I can't keep my mouth shut. "Well, you *don't* want her muffins. Besides, Pretzel Power at the Galleria has been closed for months. I think the only place they're still open is Rich Hill Mall."

Why did I have to say anything? Now the Laci spotlight is shining directly on me. She's three seconds away from asking me to go get her pretzels.

"Rich Hill Mall. That's not far," she says. "I'll bet my mom will take me."

Toby leans forward so he's between me and Laci. I'm ready to thank him when he goes completely out of his mind. "You can't go there, Laci. Especially not with your mom! Remember the mall napper? You know he's struck Rich Hill Mall like ten times."

Jeez. If I could only tell him the mall napper's been caught, I could take Toby's freak-out down a notch or two. But the funny thing is, Laci isn't having any of it. "Look, Toby," she says, "I'm not scared of spending five minutes at a mall. My mom says we shouldn't let a guy like that stop us from living our lives. If we do, it's like *we're* being held hostage. Besides, the police will catch him soon." Everybody's staring as she snakes her neck around Toby and speaks directly to me. "So, our meeting starts at seven thirty. Do you know if the mall's open that early?"

I shake my head, not wanting to get even more involved, but I have to tell her. "You can't show up that morning. You have to call and see if they can do it. Like, at my grandmother's diner, they'll do that sort of stuff for customers—as long as they know ahead of time. The bakers *hate* it when somebody shows up at six a.m. with a last-minute order of a hundred sticky buns, or something."

Laci nods enthusiastically. "I never thought of that. Thanks, Clayton." She reaches out and squeezes my shoulder, then tilts her head without taking her green eyes off me. "Thanks, you guys."

And she's gone.

Toby looks at me, his eyes narrowed and his mouth open.

Okay, I'm confused. "What?"

He shakes his head. "You really do hate her."

I raise my eyebrows. " 'Hate' is overkill, don't you think? I was trying to help her out; why are your panties in a wad?"

Toby's whole forehead is squeezed tight. "Help her? I doubt it. Why would you send her to Rich Hill Mall? Or *any* mall?"

"Because that's where the pretzels are. Why else? And you heard her. Her mom isn't worried about the mall napper and neither is she. Seriously, Toby, you're starting to sound paranoid."

"What do you mean? You know how many people he's robbed. Don't you care? The napper has a gun, Clayton. A real gun. Laci could get hurt."

Care? I care more than anyone. And I can't believe Toby actually thinks I would purposely send Laci to the mall to get kidnapped.

I stifle a groan. Part of me wants to shout out what the whole world will finally know when the police have their press conference this afternoon: the mall napper is behind bars. Who knew keeping my big mouth shut would be the hardest part of this job?

And something else is bothering me, too. "Since when do you care so much about Laci Peters?"

Toby stands and picks up his tray and walks away, his cheeks flushed red, and that's when I know for sure something is up.

I shrug at the guys, who are watching us with grins, and dash after Toby. I look up at the clock. Gran told me the police press conference is supposed to be at one o'clock—and it's only twelve.

All I can think as I catch up to him is, Could sixty minutes matter that much? "Hey, man, I heard they got the guy, so you don't have to worry about it, okay?"

Toby stops, his eyebrows locked together. "The napper? They got him? Are you sure?"

"Yeah," I say. "I got some kind of news text on my phone—I don't know. But they definitely got him."

He stares a few feet away to where Laci is talking with one of her friends. His shoulders sag and he turns back to me. I watch his eyes return to Laci like a lovesick puppy, and now I know it's true. He likes her.

"Okay, then I guess there's no problem," he says, his feet reluctantly moving with mine toward the cafeteria doors.

I open my mouth to speak, then close it.

Toby's wrong. There *is* a problem. Only, it has nothing to do with pretzels or the mall napper.

It has to do with Laci Peters.

CHAPTER TEN

I'm heading out to the field. Warm-ups don't start till three thirty, but Toby and I like to shoot a little before the field gets crowded.

I take my bag and jog midway to the goal, then grab my favorite stick and knuckle the weave of the pocket, scanning the fence line; but it's not Toby I see.

There's a man in a black suit leaning against the fence, watching me from behind dark sunglasses.

What is *he* doing here?

When the captain sees I've noticed him, he pushes off the fence, and the way he rumbles across the field, I feel like I'm a kid in trouble.

Finally, he stops in front of me, his shiny black shoes glistening even brighter from his walk through the damp grass. And as my eyes rise to his face, I notice his grim expression. Every one of my muscles tightens, and I ask the question I've been wondering about all afternoon.

"How was the news conference?"

He grunts and looks past me, removing the glasses and tucking them into his breast pocket. "Canceled."

"Canceled?" I can't believe it. "Why?"

He shakes his head and spins, taking the whole place in. The drizzly morning has turned into a sunny afternoon, and for April, it's pretty warm. "So, Clayton, you play lacrosse." It's not a question.

I twirl my stick. "Yeah."

He nods. "Your grandfather was my coach in college."

I almost drop my stick. "Really?" I look hard at the captain, trying to put this together. He worked with Gramps, and played for him, too. So why hadn't I ever seen the man before?

There's something weird between the captain and my family, and no matter how much I wrack my brain, I can't figure it out. It seems like I should know stuff like this.

But one thing *does* make sense. "So that's why you thought of me when you needed a kid."

"Yup," he says. "And, Clayton, I'm here because we need you again."

A warning shot of adrenaline whistles through my veins. "You—need me again? Because you didn't find the senator's wife and daughter?"

"That's right. But thanks to you, we started taking a hard look at the physical descriptions, and now we're getting closer. You see, even though they've tried to make it seem like one man, we figured out that it's a ring. Our latest theory is that they work in pairs."

I know I should be paying attention, but I sort of didn't hear much after those three words. "Thanks to me?" I say, and biting my grin, I bend to my bag and pick up a ball.

"Yes, thanks to you." He ambles over to my gear bag and picks up my spare stick, then jogs a few yards away and holds it out for a catch. Huh. The stick doesn't look out of place in his hands, even in his dress-for-success suit. I toss the ball to him and he casually tosses it back. "What's your number, Clayton?"

I throw a little harder. "Twelve."

He takes his stick back and hesitates for a second before he returns the pass, and I think I know why. It was Gramps's number.

"Yeah, I've been waiting for it. The guy who used to wear it is in high school now." I let the next one fly. "What was yours?"

"Eight," he says, catching it.

Eight. It's weird how important jersey numbers become. Most guys get a number and do their best to hold on to it—forever.

We throw back and forth, and finally I wing the ball hard. "Are you going to tell me what happened?"

He nods. "Our intelligence people have been working with the local law enforcement offices," he says, throwing a strong one right back to me. "There are several branches to deal with, because each of the malls hit has been located in a different jurisdiction. The Meldons were taken from the Galleria, for instance.

"Anyway, when I told my people that Wheeler was left-handed, it didn't fit with some of the evidence they'd collected. Then we noticed that although all the physical descriptions were similar, there were differences. So we started putting together a theory based on the assumption that it's more than one man."

We keep throwing. The captain's ball is smooth and controlled—he's holding back. He doesn't have to tell me Gramps taught him that. "The bottom line is, the senator received a ransom call this morning; unfortunately, they turned off the phone before we could trace it. We need to move on this—so we came up with a plan that includes you."

A plan. That includes me.

I whip a wild one at him, and he keeps talking as he makes a seriously respectable catch. "We want to tempt them with the same sort of kidnap victims as Mary Lou and Amber. Wealthy people they can use for more ransom."

Mary Lou and Amber. For some reason, first names make the senator's wife and daughter seem a lot more real. "So you think they're probably alive."

The captain's face stays neutral. "So far."

"And you want me to really get kidnapped, too—not like before?" My stomach feels queasy.

He nods back at me. "We'd like to try."

"But what about Wheeler? Can't he tell you anything?"

"He finally admitted that somebody hired him—told him what to do, and what to wear—and he was supposed to get a piece of the cash. He had no ID, and his fingerprints aren't in the system." The big man snorts and then adds, "Well, now they are."

My brain is still spinning, searching for possible alternatives. "But what about his—"

The captain cuts me off as if he knows what I'm going to say. "He didn't carry a cell phone, so we can't check those records. The gun's serial number was wiped clean, making it difficult to track."

Oh, yeah. The gun. For a second I can actually feel it pressed against my neck again. I shudder the thought away and focus on what the captain's saying. "...They've never found a vehicle at any of the malls, so we figure there's got to be a partner to drive it away after the assault is made. Plus, so far, no mall camera has caught anything. Whoever is running this operation is smart, Clayton—but they're hiring thugs like Wheeler, who aren't so smart. If we're not careful, these clowns could turn kidnapping into a business, like they've done with the ATM racket."

Tossing the ball is the only thing keeping my pulse steady. Finally, the captain shrugs. "They'll keep it going until we stop them. Yesterday they struck again."

Crud. Again? "Where?"

"Silver Spring," says the captain, clearing his throat. "But this mom and her little boy were lucky. A bystander was near enough to see what was going on, and far enough away not to get in the middle of it. She yelled at the mom and kid and our guy ran. It was close, though."

"So what do you think? Would the guy have taken them to an ATM, or kidnapped or murdered them?"

He shrugs again. "Anything could have happened. In the past few weeks, they've gotten away with thousands of dollars. Now they're asking for a million in ransom from the senator. If they get it, what do you think they'll do? Their pattern has been broken and is escalating by the day. Not only with the kidnapping, but now we've got one of their men. It's like aiming at a moving target."

We've stopped throwing, and the captain approaches me.

"When do you need me?" I say.

He puts one hand on my shoulder and points with the stick to the parking lot. "We're ready to brief you right now. Depending on how quickly we can get things in place, we could stage it today and keep setting up the rest of the week if we need to."

"Right now? Even if Gran said yes, there's no way I can miss practice today!" Coach would totally bench me—if he didn't kick me off the team. And the guys would kill me if that happened. "Captain, I might be in seventh grade, but we only have two eighth graders, and they're both on defense. It's me and Toby who score most of the goals."

"I get that. And I know what a team expects from its players—so help me figure this out. Because what we're dealing with is a very different scoreboard. It's about people's lives." The captain pauses as he grabs my lacrosse stick and examines the shaft, comparing it to my backup. Then he looks straight into my eyes. "There are thousands of people who are alive and well today because members of your family stopped terror in its tracks. And you have the opportunity to carry on their work."

He waits in silence as I dig deep for the Save the World chromosome the Stone family seems to carry in abundance. Captain Thompson turns and gazes across the field at the parking lot. "You have games this week?"

I sigh. "Biggest of the season. Tomorrow and Friday. If we win both, we have a good shot in the play-offs."

"What time?"

"Seven tomorrow, and four on Friday."

The captain's lips move to the side of his face like he's adding numbers. "Let's take this one step at a time," he says. "If we take you out of school early tomorrow, we could get you to your game on time—no guarantees, but it's possible." He thumps my shoulder and hands my stick back to me. "What do you say, Clayton?"

If I don't do it, who will?

"Okay. But considering what happened last time, don't you think I need something more than a sedative stick?"

The captain stifles a smile. "Don't worry. I'll talk to our guy and have him start working on some special items, specifically for you."

Huh. "Like my own gun?"

He shakes his head and almost laughs. "I'm afraid that after the sedative stick fiasco, a gun is out of the question for a long while. Besides, your grandmother's right. You'd need months of training." Then he hesitates and looks toward the fence line. Toby's got his gear slung over his shoulder and is jogging our way. "But there are other options."

Toby's approaching fast; he's squinting, as if he's trying to figure out who I'm talking to.

In one casual move, Captain Thompson tucks his stick into my bag and slips his sunglasses back on. "So you practice now, and I'll talk to your grandmother and see if I can pick you up later."

I don't even have the "Sure" out of my mouth before his back is turned and he's heading for the parking lot. He doesn't acknowledge Toby as he blows by, but Toby is sure getting a load of him. I guess the black suit and buffed shoes do look a little out of place.

"Who was that?"

"That?" I say.

Toby rolls his eyes. "Who else?" His tone tells me he's still not over the scene with Laci.

"Uh, a friend of my grandmother's."

I watch Toby turn and stare at the captain, who's stepping into the backseat of the gleaming black Suburban. "*That's* who you were with Sunday?"

Swallowing, I nod.

"He looks important. Who is he?"

What do I say to that? I settle on the truth, but the sort of truth that will reroute the conversation. "My grandfather was his lacrosse coach in college."

Sure enough, that does it. I can almost see Toby's brain chug down a different track. "Really?"

The Suburban pulls away, and I turn to my best friend. I want to make everything right between us. Go back to the way it was three days ago, before I had to lie every thirty seconds. When lacrosse and my friends, and Toby, were the most important things in my life.

I toss my ball in the air a couple of times, and even though things have been a little tense between us, Toby knows what's coming as I pull my stick back.

He reaches down to his open bag, and by the time the ball blazes out of my pocket, his stick is ready—and he catches it, no problem.

He always has.

CHAPTER ELEVEN

Practice runs late, and for the last half hour I'm distracted looking for the captain's Suburban. It never shows, and as I'm walking toward the lot, I don't know whether I'm relieved or bummed to see Gran's white Lexus instead.

I toss my gear in her trunk—she won't let it in the car because she says it stinks worse than flattened skunk—and hop in the front seat.

"We're going to the diner," she says.

My legs are sore and I sorta feel like going home, but whatever. When Gran has a busy day, we usually end up at the diner for dinner. "I could go for one of Gramps's specials," I say.

"Why don't you call ahead so they have it ready? I need to talk to you about something."

I was going to ask about the captain, but I'm glad I didn't. I'd rather not get Gran riled while my stomach is growling for food.

We arrive at Big Stone's in record time, and something about the way Gran cranks the steering wheel and yanks the gearshift into park tells me that whatever conversation she had with Captain Thompson didn't go very well.

I follow her as she marches up the concrete steps and into the restaurant Gramps designed to look like a titanic silver bullet. She whips past the front cash register, and as we pass our favorite booth, I'm beginning to realize this will not be a regular "talk." Am I in trouble? Is she gonna yell?

The three cooks at the open grill don't even look up as we pass through the galley. It's the dinner rush, and it smells amazing. Every single food in that kitchen—warm maple syrup, baked cinnamon apples, stewed tomatoes, cheese melting over crisp home fries, charbroiled rib eye steaks, garlic bread—hits my nose at once and comforts me for a second as I take in the sight like I'm five years old again. Pans are sizzling and sauces and soups are steaming from enormous pots, and plates are sliding back and forth across the long stainless steel counter. I see an oversized bacon cheeseburger sitting on a tray at the very end and yell, "Hey, Carlos! Is that mine?"

The head cook looks up from the pot he's stirring and nods. "Hey, Clayton. *Sí*, that is yours. French fries, well done, just for you." His dramatic Spanish accent makes all food, even French fries, sound exotic.

Carlos always remembers what I like. He puts extra malt in my milk shakes, sizzles my fries until they're a deep golden brown and warms my three-berry pie.

I pick up the tray. He also remembers what I don't like. The famous pickles. He made sure to put the biggest one he could find right beside my burger. "Still not funny," I say, and start toward my grandmother's office.

Carlos winks as he wipes his hands on the towel draped over his shoulder, then moves to another bubbling pot. "Maybe not to you."

I make my way through the dimly lit hallway and enter Gran's office. Just as I'm about to put my tray on top of some papers, she waves me over to Gramps's old desk. She hasn't let me, or anybody, sit there since he died, and she hasn't touched it, either. Every single thing is exactly the way he left it, from the oversized tomato tin filled with pens, pencils and Sharpies, to the calendar marked with scribbles and doodles and appointments he made—right up to that very last day. The only thing that's new is the dust.

My eyes are caught briefly by Gramps's business card holder, still full. I can practically see him finger one and casually slip it to a visiting salesman. I bend forward and for the first time, actually read the card.

Jack P. Stone

703-555-1939   **At Your Service**

"Sit," Gran says, pointing to his chair.

I put my tray down and sit, and then I eat in silence while Gran stares at me. There's not a whole lot to look at as I chew and avoid Gran's intense gaze. The room is crammed with file cabinets, bookcases and piles of papers stacked on top of both enormous wooden desks. An organized mess is what she calls it.

When I push back from my almost-empty tray, I look up to meet Gran's narrowed eyes. She shakes her head. "What is wrong with that pickle?"

"Gran, you know I hate—"

She leaps out of her chair and comes toward me, still shaking her head. "Why can't you appreciate a good pickle?" she says, snatching it from my plate and taking a bite. She points the rest of it at me. "These pickles will pay for your college education, young man. It was a happy accident the day your grandfather stumbled on the recipe—and that people loved them so much that Premier Pickles paid quite a price for it, and they continue to pay. You should *love* these pickles." Then she takes another bite, practically daring me to argue.

"Gramps didn't *love* the pickles."

Gran stops chewing. "Precisely. He didn't—and you see what happened to him?"

My grandmother is nuts. "He drowned, Gran. I don't think a pickle could have saved him."

"Probably not." She shakes the last of the pickle at me, and an unwilling smile cracks her cheeks. "But he would have had better digestion."

I grin back at her. It's the exact sort of argument she would have with Gramps. And then I remember why we're here. "So you wanted to talk to me about what? Pickles?"

Gran freezes. "Oh, yes," she says through instantly thin lips. I can tell she's getting ready to dump something major on me, probably to do with Captain Thompson.

Instead of spilling, though, she goes to the door, slams it shut and starts throwing dead bolts from the top of the door to the bottom—locks I never even noticed until this second. Next thing I know, she's reaching underneath her desk, pulling out a footstool. I don't have time to wonder what the heck she needs a footstool for, because in one astounded blink of my eyes, she's ducked inside her small supply closet and is doing a little pirouette on the stool like a ballerina in order to reach...to reach *what*?

Whatever it is, it's near the ceiling. After a series of jumps and spins that would probably kill anyone except an ex-dancer, her ceiling-fiddling is done and she steps down and looks at me, exhaling a long, satisfied sigh.

"All right, Clayton. Come with me."

I move slightly forward in my chair, not quite sure how she expects us to go anywhere with the office door bolted. "Come where?"

She steps back into the supply closet and raps the wall. "In here, of course."

I was kidding earlier when I said Gran was nuts. Now I'm not so sure. "I thought you told me never to go into a closet with anyone."

"Very funny. Get in here."

I don't know why, but I do what she says. I stand up and, step by tentative step, make my way toward her.

"Clayton! Please get moving. That's a good young man." She reaches out and clasps my arm with her hand. "I know it's cramped, but it's necessary for a moment."

She shuts the closet door with her free hand and there's utter darkness. Being shoved against anyone in such a small room, er, closet, is one thing, but it's my *grandmother*—a second later she lets go of my arm and is back to her gymnastic routine. Something knocks me hard in the ribs; her foot? "Gran! What are you doing?"

"One—more—switch," she says, grunting each syllable. "Your grandfather made this so complicated; he didn't want anyone to figure it out."

A wrenching noise of scraping metal reverberates from the right wall, and my eyes are drawn to a sudden, bright stream of light cracking across the floor. I squint and look hard, trying to take in what I'm seeing. 'Cause I swear the wall is opening.

I instinctively take a step back and reach for the doorknob, but at the same time, I'm over-the-top curious. A glare overwhelms my vision, and the closet's side wall is, well, it's not there anymore.

"It's all right, Clayton," says Gran, pulling at my arm again. "Get in."

All I see is white glare. "Get in? Get in what?"

"Why, the elevator, of course. Can't you see it?"

I blink and look hard, forcing my eyes to adjust. There *is* an elevator. I inch forward, and I know my mouth is hanging open but I can't help it. Wow. Brushed steel rails outline gleaming wood panels, and the ceiling is cranking enough light to fill a whole house.

"An elevator, Gran?" I say from inside the box. There's a pretty tight control panel to my left, and it occurs to me: "Where does it go?"

Gran flicks my shoulder with her finger. "Oh, come on, Clayton. It doesn't go up...."

No second floor on the diner. I guess that was a stupid question.

I turn to Gran with a more appreciative eye. I never saw this coming. "So can I at least ask where *we're* going?"

Gran sticks her finger in a slot next to the control panel and does some ninja finger move on the keyboard. Without looking at me, she holds out her hand. "Give me your index finger."

I respond with one of Gramps's old jokes. *"How would you like it? Sliced, chopped, or julienned?"*

Gran groans and faces me. "Must you?" she says, grabbing my hand. "Clayton, if you are serious about helping the Special Service, I suggest you take this exercise more to heart." Then she separates my index finger from the rest of me—ouch!—and sticks it in the little slot. "Press down, but gently."

I do, and a second later the wall closes and we're moving. Or the elevator is.

I don't have time to think before the door is opening again. Gran steps toward it, still holding my arm. "Let's go."

I follow her out of the elevator, still in a state of semishock. The room in front of us is football-stadium enormous, and I turn to my grandmother and raise my eyebrows.

She smiles and shrugs. "Clayton, I've got a few things to tell you about our past—and your future."

I can't speak.

So I follow her.

CHAPTER TWELVE

Gran's heels snap against the polished concrete floor as she whisks across the vast room. It's like entering a world I've only seen on a movie screen. Like in *Star Trek* or the *Iron Man* movies. The only thing I can compare it to in real life is Mission Control at NASA—Gramps took me there once—but that's puny compared to this.

My grandmother pauses about midway through the room, and this time, she raises her eyebrows at me. "Well, what do you think?"

I look from one end of the room to the other. Computer panels and screens wrap the perimeter at eye level, with another row cutting through the center of the room, people in dark suits bent quietly over each monitor. Above the computers, floor-to-ceiling maps of the United States and the entire globe flash information like current weather or air traffic. Then, higher still, probably twenty of the most ginormous flat-panels I've ever seen are set to news channels all over the world, with closed-captioning in English, Spanish and Chinese.

I turn to Gran, gasping for my voice. "So, you obviously get cable down here."

Gran replies, straight-faced, "Yes, we're more than adequately wired for cable. We even have our own satellites."

I can't believe what I'm seeing, what's been beneath me all these years. "Gran, how big is this place?"

"Oh, well, of course we're under the diner, and the parking lot, and the grocery store next door...."

I shake my head, watching the people working, and I totally get something else. "There's got to be another way down here."

Gran laughs. "Actually, there are several. You were here two days ago, only you entered though a building five blocks away. Our elevators are more like high-tech subway cars, although you'd never know it by riding in them, would you?"

I'm too stunned to reply—this place must be *huge*.

"Have you ever noticed anything unusual about booth thirteen?"

A prickly feeling runs straight across my shoulders. "What is it, a trapdoor?"

"Something like that."

Then I remember seeing people mysteriously appear from the enclosed area out back. "And behind the Dumpsters?"

Gran smiles and nods. "Oh, yes. And you know the parking garage behind the grocery?"

I knew it. "It's part of this place?"

"Most of it."

Gran reclaims my arm and leads me to a cluster of empty chairs and couches. She signals with her free hand to somebody I can't see. "Let's go over here and have something to drink— and a small chat. Things have gone a little haywire today."

I sit in a leather chair and rub its soft arms. "So you talked to Captain Thompson? You know there's a problem."

Her lips are thin again. "Yes." She turns to a lady heading our way with a glass of ice, a Coke can and a mug of coffee. The woman sets the drinks down on the table in front of us.

"Uh, thanks."

Gran picks up her mug and takes a small sip. "Clayton, this is Frankie. She works here."

Frankie smiles at me. To Gran, she says, "Anything else, ma'am?"

"Not right now, Frankie."

Then the lady disappears behind a wall so quickly, I swear she walked right through it.

"Gran," I say, flipping the Coke tab open. "What's going on?"

"First we need to clear up some details. I spoke to Derek, er, Captain Thompson, and he is very interested in continuing a relationship between you and the Special Service. You have been a great help already. But before you officially commit yourself, I want to make a few things perfectly clear. As we have discussed, undercover work is a risky business."

I take a sip and it sort of chokes me on the way down. She said "officially commit." I have no idea what she's talking about, so I nod and let her keep going.

"Although I'm not sure I agree, Captain Thompson seems to think your natural instincts are well suited to this work and you'll make a good agent one day." She briefly closes her eyes and shakes her head. "Clayton, I am your grandmother and sole guardian, so forgive me if struggle with the prospect of knowingly putting you in danger. I simply don't want you to—"

I fill in the missing word, because it's stuck; she won't let it past her lips. "Die?"

She gives a little *humph*. "Exactly."

I shake my head back at her. "Gran, *it's not all about me.*" We both freeze when I say it. Even though it's true—it's *not* about me—those aren't my words.

Her shoulders tense, getting ready for whatever is about to come out of my mouth next. My shoulders aren't so relaxed, either. The memory of Gramps lives in this place, and we both know it.

And somehow, he's the one who gives me the guts to keep talking. "The last place I want to be is in the backseat with some crazy dude. But how else are we going to help Amber and her mom?"

Gran lets out a long breath and tilts her head, like she's challenging me. "What are you saying, Clayton?"

What am I saying? "That there's only one thing to do. Only one thing I *can* live with."

"Okay, then," she says, standing, her voice defiant. "It looks like I have no choice, either."

"What do you mean?"

She walks to a spot a few yards beyond where we've been sitting and sticks her finger inside a tiny, hardly visible notch in the wall. Without turning, she gestures for me to follow, and for the second time today, I wonder where the heck we're going. Until the wall starts to divide and opens to reveal an entire room lined floor to ceiling with huge rectangles of white marble. Really? I mean, *really?*

Huge framed pictures and certificates and medals decorate the room, and an American flag stands on display in the corner. There's a long ebony conference table on the left and a seating area with a couch and a few chairs on the right. My gaze floats to the back of the room, where a serious desk sits—bigger and nicer than anything I've seen in my life. It's an office for some mega-bigwig. Like a president, or something.

I watch Gran walk slowly to the back of the room and make her way around the desk, running her finger across it like she's checking for dust. And when she sits in the big leather chair behind it, a huge feeling of pride begins to pump up my chest. Gramps. He was the big shot around here. Maybe that's why I feel him so strongly.

"Clayton, I have something to tell you. And it may change everything," says Gran. "Your grandfather worked here."

Well, duh.

"But he wasn't in charge of all this."

Oh. Then why—

She meets my eyes and clears her throat.

"I was."

CHAPTER THIRTEEN

I stare at Gran and rewind those last words. Did I hear right? Gramps's boss? *Everybody's* boss?

She sinks into the black leather chair like it's an old friend. And the picture in my head refocuses. This is my grandmother. She hollers at cooks and waitresses at Big Stone's. She makes roast chicken and baked potato soup. And beds. She makes beds.

She gets out of her chair, walks around the desk and puts her arms around me before she speaks again. "Oh, Clayton, we knew we'd have to explain someday. But when your grandfather retired two years ago, to watch over you while your parents were overseas, you weren't old enough to understand. And then we got the news—"

A hundred emotions I squash down every single day—anger, hurt, confusion—instantly flush through my bloodstream like boiling water, and I barely stop myself from screaming. There are more secrets. More lies.

"Mom and Dad. *You* sent them away."

Gran hugs me hard. "I'm sorry, Clayton."

I don't understand. "But how could you do that?"

"My job—" She stops midsentence and shakes her head, like she doesn't understand, either. "I can share only the broadest details, for security reasons. But that operation required penetration into a particularly difficult area that had been infiltrated by double agents. Local citizens had lost almost all control of their city, their land and their lives."

She looks away. "Because of their skills, your mother and father were uniquely qualified to immerse themselves as trusted members of the community." There's a long pause before she finishes. "They were the best fit for the mission; we all knew that."

I'm trying really hard to not make this about me, except all I want to do is shout, *Doesn't anyone care about* me?

As if she can read my mind, Gran turns back to me and lifts my chin with her index finger. "The only way your parents would take the assignment was if your grandfather agreed to retire and keep you safe."

I fall into a chair, baffled. The life I thought I had never existed. It's like everybody around me has been wearing masks, and one by one, they've been taking them off. Will life ever be normal again? Gramps is gone. My parents are gone. And Gran. I look up at her. She's—what is she?

Gran sweeps her hand around the presidential office. "I left this job when we lost your parents. Things were getting risky for me here, and I thought it was what they would have wanted me to do. When your grandfather died so suddenly, I knew I'd made the right choice."

I take it all in. The desk, the sleek-looking artwork; my eyes make their way around the expansive room, finally resting on the American flag. "So why are we—I mean, what—" I don't quite know what I'm asking.

Gran shrugs and follows my gaze around the office. "Well, for one thing, I'm going back to work."

I sit straight up. "Uh, Gran, you've been retired for over a year. Isn't somebody else in charge now?"

Gran sighs, still not looking at me. "They filled the position, yes. Unfortunately, he never started. . . ." Her voice trails off.

All my confusion and resentment are instantly wiped out by her announcement. "What do you mean?"

"Clayton, you must understand, the president requested we get involved in the mall napper crimes only because of the senator and his family. In general, the Special Service provides undercover support to organizations like the CIA, the FBI and all branches of the military. We help fallen leaders, scientists and double agents escape from their countries and into asylum. We are called on to steal secrets or prototypes of weapons that could threaten the United States. And—we are called on to do things I will never tell you about."

She narrows her eyes. "So there are people who would like to put the Special Service out of business—everyone from international politicians and businesspeople to terrorists." She stops talking for a moment and leans close, forcing me to look into her eyes. "This job is not suited to everyone."

She gives me a moment to consider what she's saying before continuing. "You say the word, Clayton, and we can both get back in that elevator and leave this behind. For good. This time, the decision is yours."

Is that true? Can we do that? "But that would mean—"

Gran cuts me off. "It would mean we fill the elevator shaft with concrete, I run the diner until I die of natural causes at the age of one hundred and ten, and you live the rest of your childhood playing every sport under the sun and listening to lectures every time your report card arrives. *That's* what it would mean."

I stare at her. She's right. It would mean I wouldn't have to be so scared. It would mean Gran would be safe. It would mean I wouldn't miss any lacrosse practices or games. It would mean I wouldn't have to hide things from my friends.

And then there are the other things it would mean. It would mean not helping the Special Service or Captain Thompson. It would mean some mom or kid might get robbed or even die in the next few days. And maybe more moms and more kids, in the weeks ahead.

I've made my decision, only it feels like I made it a long time ago. Maybe even before I was born. Sure, I'm not a good agent yet, but the captain thinks I could be—someday.

I cock my head toward my grandmother. "I kinda like the elevator, Gran. So I guess we just have to nail the nappers."

With a nod and a small smile, she spins in place, and in three powerful strides she's at the very back of her office. She signals for me to follow as she turns the corner and disappears through an open corridor.

CHAPTER FOURTEEN

I run to catch up, and as I turn the corner, it's like a scene from a movie. With each click-clack of Gran's shoes, lights flick awake, turning absolute darkness into light.

She stops, a black wall of nothing in front of her, and turns left to face a garage-like door. Then she presses the button on a miniature remote and winks at me as the door opens, exposing a closet the size of a tractor-trailer. "This is where I keep my personal stash," she says, as if she's referring to her secret chocolate drawer that Gramps never knew about.

But what I'm looking at aren't shelves of chocolate. Is she planning a war? This is not an everyday collection of self-defense gadgets—it's an all-out science fiction armory.

My heart begins to thump as she leads me to the far corner and rummages in one of the shelves. She turns around with what appears to be a small cannon in her hand, lifting it so I can have a full view. Her eyes sparkle with—glee? She wasn't this excited when the new jukebox arrived at the diner, and she waited six months for that!

"Gran, is that a cannon?"

She smiles. "Sort of. We can attach it to a vehicle, or a building—anything, really—and operate it by remote. This darling fires balls filled with electric currents, and it can be set on a range from stun to deadly force. They strike their target, poof! Gone. No evidence of munitions. It's one of my favorites."

Her eyes drift farther down the shelves, and she gives a little gasp as she flings the cannon back on its shelf and runs like a schoolgirl to pick up, what? A miniature fighter jet?

About thirty-seven thousand nine hundred and twenty-four hairs prickle like centipedes crawling down my neck. "Does it fly?"

"For two billion research dollars over the last five years, he *better* fly," she says, stroking the jet like it's the pet Yorkie she never had. "We can send this little guy anywhere, even across an ocean. His range is unlimited because he uses solar panels to constantly recharge his lithium batteries." She pauses and looks at me with a sigh. "But you need to have top secret clearance before I can tell you what he does."

Is this the same person who struggles to turn the television on at home? Or is that all part of her cover? One thing's for sure. Gran is a gadget hound. "Are we gonna use it?"

She returns my gaze, and her eyes dim. "I guess not," she says, and puts the plane back on the shelf. "But one of these days he'll be just what we need." Then she reaches up to a hook on the wall and grabs a small black duffel bag. "We bring what is necessary. Nothing more, nothing less. But I should probably stock up at home, too. Just in case."

She moves quickly from one shelf to the next, randomly selecting weapons, gadgets and other gear, tucking them inside the padded bag and securing each in its own compartment. I watch her, thinking, *In case?* In case what?

Gran looks me up and down and then moves to another shelf and reaches on tiptoes for a box. She opens it, brings down something tiny, looks it over, fiddles with it for a minute and then hands it to me. "This is for tomorrow."

I hold it in my hand, not sure what to say. "Uh, Gran. I already have a pen."

She cranks her left eyebrow at me. "You are a child, Clayton. What do you expect us to give you? I assure you, you can be effective without bullets." She gestures to the pen. "It's like the cannon I showed you, but more, shall we say, manageable."

I look from my pen to Gran's duffel bag. For a second, I imagine what it would feel like to stop a bad guy with a real weapon. Then I shrug. I guess I have to start somewhere. I twist my new toy in my hand. "Thanks."

"I limited your distance to three feet and set it to an intermediate stun level. It shoots precisely, like a laser, so aim is important."

I nod. "Where do I keep it?"

She thinks a minute before deciding. "Right now it's turned off, so it will be fine in your pocket. We'll meet Captain Thompson later tonight, to go over the specifics, how to load a charge and shoot it. We also need to discuss the plan for tomorrow."

They already have a plan? "Are we going back to a mall?"

Gran nods as she zips her loaded bag closed. "Yes, but it's more complicated this time. There's a clean air fund-raiser this week, and Ina Klum, an old friend, is supposed to be in town for it. She's a big contributor to the senator's campaign, but she's rarely seen. So she's agreed to help us out by staying home and lying low. I'll be taking her place at the press conference tomorrow—with you by my side, playing the role of her grandson."

What? "Say again?"

"Clayton, this is what the Special Service does. We go undercover, disguise ourselves. By tomorrow afternoon, no one will be able to tell me from Ina Klum. And *you* will make a very convincing grandson who—"

A startling squeak of rubber hitting linoleum sounds behind me and I shut down the urge to jump three feet out of my skin. Gran doesn't even flinch; she looks past me and motions with her free hand. "Jones. Good. Please come in. Did you bring what you need?"

I turn to see a tall, skinny, young-looking guy—I mean, seriously, he could be in high school—wearing a geeky white lab coat and a black-and-white checkered bandana tied around his head. Sweat is beaded on his forehead, like he ran two miles to get here.

Jones holds up a metal briefcase, also black-and-white checkered. "Chief," he says, with a slight roll of his eyes, "have you ever known me to arrive unprepared?"

I spin back to Gran. There's a tiny smirk at the edge of her mouth, and her eyebrows are raised. "February 6, 2014. April 13, 2012. June 15, 2011. Would you like me to go on?"

Jones groans like this squabble is a rerun he could recite in his sleep, and the response bursts from his lips like automatic fire. "Blizzard followed by the coldest day on record—*everybody's* equipment froze. A flat tire on the Fourteenth Street Bridge during rush hour—wouldn't have had to use your precious cannon if the Service van had its own jack. And my high school graduation—did you really expect me to erase milestone pictures on that memory card for a dead body photo shoot? My mom would have killed me!"

Gran shakes her head and laughs. She puts her hand on my shoulder. "Jones, I want you to meet my grandson, Clayton. We'll call him a junior decoy for now, but the bottom line is, he needs a wrap. A good one. By tomorrow."

"Gotcha covered," Jones says to Gran. He opens his briefcase, pulls out a device that looks like a small rectangular flashlight and points it at me. It starts flashing. "So, Clayton—finally getting into the family business."

"I guess," I say, trying to understand what's going on, and why he's zapping my body with beams of blue light. "A wrap?"

My grandmother begins to explain, "A wrap is—" until Jones waves her off.

"Let the professional handle it."

Gran raises an eyebrow but lets the guy talk while he works on me. "A wrap is like a bulletproof vest, only it's fitted to your entire body like an extra layer of skin. We developed it using the latest nanotechnology. Do you play any sports?"

I nod.

"You wear Under Armour?"

"Sure."

"Well, it feels like that when you wear it, except it can withstand electrical shocks and deflect a decent range of residual shrapnel, especially if you're not right on top of whatever is exploding. It also acts as a flotation device. Most people in this business wear one at all times; a wrap is ideal for undercover work because it's not so obvious. Anyone in backup or attack mode wears a standard-issue vest that does a better job of shielding major organs and deflecting heavy-duty ammo. Eventually, we'll be making this wrap even stronger than those, but that's at least a year away."

I remember back to when Wheeler had his gun pressed into my neck. "So, a wrap isn't gonna do me any good if somebody has a gun here . . . ?" I gesture to the general area of my head.

Jones shrugs. "At close range, you're out of luck no matter where they point it. You'll get deflection from a distance, depending on the type of bullet, though."

Note to self: figure out a way to avoid bullets in general.

He shuts his briefcase and turns back to Gran. "Is that all?"

"For now," she says with a nod. "Good to see you, Jones. And thank you."

He opens his mouth but stops midword. Instead, he shrugs and smiles back at her, walking away. Just as he approaches the door, he turns. "I knew you'd be back," he says.

Before Gran can respond, he's gone.

CHAPTER FIFTEEN

I hustle up the steps and into school just as the first round of morning announcements is starting. Toby's waiting, and after I stick my banana in my backpack, he hands me my mocha.

"Ready for the game?" he says as we make our way to Mr. Davis's classroom.

I gulp the hot coffee, but with each swallow, an even hotter guilt is filling me. We're supposed to be in the locker room by six o'clock tonight. Warm-ups start at six thirty. The game is at seven. And the chances of me making any of those times are slim as Jim.

I don't meet Toby's eyes and try to sidetrack what I already know is going to be an impossible conversation. "Runner's getting a lot better."

Mission accomplished. Toby's head starts vibrating like a tortured bobble-head doll. "Clayton, the only thing that's gonna help Runner's pocket is superglue. This is an important game, and..." We head into Mr. Davis's classroom, and Toby continues to list all the ways Runner is not ready to play today, and how the team has to get it together.

As he takes a breath, knowing I'd better talk fast, I ask him, "Hey, after school, can you bring my bag to the locker room? I have a dentist appointment at five o'clock, so I might be a little late for warm-ups." When I turn my head, I'm staring directly into Toby's grapefruit-sized eyes.

"What? You can't show up late. You know what Coach will do. Man, you gotta cancel it. Here," he says, reaching for my face, "open your mouth."

I open.

"Like I thought. All you need is a toothbrush."

I seriously wish I could explain.

"Toby, you know if it's up to me, I'll be there on time. Okay?" That's the truth.

"Every practice, every game, Clayton. That's *you* who says that. What are you doing? I just don't get what's with you this week."

I stare back at Toby, wishing I knew if I was lying or not. "I'll be there," I say.

"Mr. Stone," Mr. Davis calls from the front of the room. He's waving an envelope in the air. "I have something for you."

Relieved to get away from Toby, I go to Mr. Davis's desk and take the envelope from him. "What is it?"

Mr. Davis raises his eyebrows. "Laci Peters delivered it a few minutes ago."

I go back to my seat and open it.

Dear Clayton:

I am excited to inform you that you have been nominated to run for Student Council Vice President at Masters Academy Middle School for next year's term. Elections will be held in three weeks. There will be a meeting Thursday morning at 7:30 in the administration conference room to discuss school policy regarding speeches, platform limitations and running alliances.

Congratulations on your nomination.
Sincerely,
Ms. Tracy Templeton
Headmistress
Masters Academy

What the heck? Me. *Me?* Who in their right mind would nominate *me?*

I look around the classroom to see if I'm being punked. But nobody's paying attention except Toby. He points a threatening finger at me, and I shrug and turn back to the letter.

Definitely not reopening that conversation.

CHAPTER SIXTEEN

The morning goes by pretty quickly, and before I know it I'm signing out and sprinting down the steps in front of school. Captain Thompson is waiting in the black Suburban.

"Hop in, Clayton," he says through the open window. "We've got a lot to do."

I get in and look around. "Where's Gran?"

The captain signals the driver to get moving and then turns to me. "She needed an early start on her transformation to Ina Klum. I'm going to brief you, in case you missed anything last night."

This is sounding official.

"These guys are watching the senator's every move, so we think this press conference should get their attention. As for the background on Mrs. Klum: She and your grandmother have been friends for years, and on occasion Ina has helped the Special Service in one way or another. She's a very wealthy woman who's funded acres and acres of windmill farms in North Dakota. She's supposed to be in DC for a fund-raiser, so your grandmother is taking her place, and you are posing as her grandson."

"The grandson is from North Dakota, too?"

The captain nods. "We've set up an operation at the airport to go over the final plans and tweak your appearance. Your flight will 'arrive' and Senator Meldon will be at the airport to greet you—accompanied by a few television cameras, of course."

I'm not getting it. "Why can't we just go to the mall like last time?"

He pulls a file from somewhere in the front seat and lays it on his lap. "That could work, but by having this press conference, it's like we're talking directly to the kidnappers. And Ina is much wealthier than the senator, so if these guys want money, Ina is their payday. We'll even drop the name of the mall you'll be visiting."

"I don't think it's going to work," I say.

Captain Thompson stares at me in silence. Finally he asks, "Why not?"

"Well, for one thing, I don't know anything about windmill farms in North Dakota, and I'm pretty sure Gran doesn't, either."

"Your grandmother can bone up on any subject in three hours. Once, she learned to speak French in two. I'll give you a brochure about windmill energy to look at, but I don't think you'll have to say much, anyway."

Huh. Gran learned French? In two hours? That's cool. But for real, all the hoopla doesn't seem right, and deep in my gut, I'm having big doubts.

"Captain," I say. "Are you sure the mall nappers and the kidnappers are the same people?"

He answers without hesitation. "Yes. Absolutely."

"Why?"

"Because of peanuts. They left shells at most of the crime scenes, including when the senator's family was taken." He sort of snorts. "Stupid, actually. They forgot about DNA."

When Agent Moxie and I got in the SUV, there were peanut shells. I gotta get better at picking up on actual clues. "Uh, Captain—"

Before I can say another word, his cell phone rings. A minute later we pull directly up to an elevator in the airport parking garage and I'm following the captain out one door and through another, into the elevator. We go down a bunch of levels and walk down white hallway after white hallway until we come to a set of frosted-glass doors, a man in a dark suit posted on either side. The men stare straight ahead and don't say a word as Captain Thompson, still holding the phone to his ear, whisks a card through a slot and the doors glide open.

"Good afternoon, gentlemen," he says to them as we pass.

Two abrupt "Sirs" echo behind us.

We come to another door that's cracked open, and Captain Thompson pushes through with me two paces behind.

We enter a long room with a low-tiled ceiling. Tables are stacked with plastic containers, fabrics and other junk peeking out from under their cockeyed lids, toolboxes filled with everything from jewelry to makeup, and portable closets lined with clothes.

The captain puts his cell back in his pocket and cranes his neck to get a closer look at something. "Chief? Is that you? I thought you were going with one of your wigs."

I move around him so I can see. Gran is sitting in a chair, everything covered but her face and hands. She's got a giant black cape tied around her neck and a plastic bag tied tight to her head, and she's surrounded by people going at her like she's a Mercedes in a car wash, including a guy who's painting her face with goo.

Gran shrugs. "Georgette will dye it back in a few days." She spots me and gestures from underneath the cape with her finger. "Let's get moving, Clayton. The team needs to get started. Did Captain Thompson tell you we're going to adjust some of your facial features?"

"Whoa! Are you kidding me?" He forgot to mention that minor detail. I turn to the captain. "Like what?"

"Not a big deal, Clayton," he says. "A little putty and makeup and pulling your skin so your cheekbones are more pronounced. A new nose, maybe ears if we have time. You'll be all over the news, and we don't want anyone to recognize you." His eyes briefly sweep the setup as he adds, "That's the entire point of all this."

"Who's gonna recognize me? My friends don't even watch the news."

Gran leans forward in her chair, and the muck on her face jiggles as she answers sternly. "Clayton, your friends are the least of our concerns."

I turn back to Captain Thompson. "You said 'tweak.' Yanking back my whole face and putting on new ears is not tweaking."

The captain and Gran exchange a look.

"Well, everything is removable, except the hair," says Captain Thompson. "Only, it has suddenly occurred to me—he can't go to school with the same hair. It's too much of a risk."

Gran nods. "What do you suggest?"

"I think Clayton just came down with the flu. That should eliminate most of his exposure to people who know him."

Gran is still nodding, agreeing.

Wait. Am I missing something? "What about my game? You said you'd try to get me there."

Captain Thompson is quiet for a second before he answers. "Clayton, the hair makes it almost impossible. If even one person notices, if they connect you to your cover—"

No. This is not right. "I'll keep my helmet on. The guys on the team would never say anything, even if they found out. Trust me. We've been keeping secrets for each other for a long time. Nobody blabs."

The captain is shaking his head. I don't know if he believes me, or what.

"Now wait a minute," says Gran. "Clayton, what if we shave your head? Then you could wear a wig—and take it off for school—and the game."

"A wig?" I hadn't thought of that. "If I wear a wig, why would I have to shave my head?"

"It's not necessary, but the adhesive will work better. We don't want to risk it falling off should things get at all physical."

I don't want to look like a freak, but if it's the game or my hair—"Okay, whatever."

Captain Thompson looks at his watch, then back at me. "It's one thirty now. The news conference footage will hit the Internet immediately, especially Twitter. We'll give it a couple of hours at Rich Hill, just to try our luck. We're setting up surveillance at every area mall, inside and out, so even if we're not successful this afternoon, maybe we can learn how they tag their targets. But, Clayton, if the nappers do attempt to take you today, all bets are off. You realize that, don't you?"

Yeah, I realize we need to get going or I for sure won't make my game. "Shave it. Glue the beaver on my head. But not so much with the ears and stuff, okay?"

Gran looks up at her "people." "You heard the boy," she says. "Let's go!"

In an instant, they've draped me with a cape, and a flurry of hands and feet and flying bodies has closed in on me. Suddenly, I'm down to my birthday suit, and before I can yell "Hey!" they're fitting me with what must be my wrap. A guy is standing to the side doing something with a pair of boxers. He answers my question even as I think it. "Backup GPS, kid. Don't want to lose you."

Two more people step forward with a new suit, shirt, tie and shoes—except for the colors, the look is suspiciously similar to my Masters uniform—and proceed to dress me under the drape like I'm three.

I furrow my brow at Captain Thompson. "Is this really necessary? I look the same." As soon as the words leave my mouth, I know I'm wrong; nothing's the same. It's all probably got bugs and cameras and who knows what else sewn into it.

When I'm totally dressed underneath the cape, the next team rushes at me with hair clippers and pushes me into my own barber chair. They're barely finished when another member of the pit crew pounces with shaving cream and a razor while a guy with a Shop-Vac sucks up all my hair from the floor.

No sooner is all my hair gone than somebody sneaks up behind me and starts slathering warm goo all over my very cold, bald head. Thirty seconds later Gran's hairdresser, Georgette, is yanking a wig onto me, pushing and pulling like she thinks I'm made of rubber. "Ow! Watch it!"

"Hold still," she says, looking intently at my new hair. After one final wrench, she steps back and studies me with a cocked head. In an instant the scissors are out and her hands are diving in and out of my hair like kamikaze fighter pilots. The Shop-Vac fires up again and the suction nozzle materializes right next to my face. The captain's right, the glue is good, because otherwise my new hair would be following my cheek up the hose.

A noxious odor seems to be accompanying a guy rolling a big cart my way. I can't see his face, 'cause, holy mother of the apocalypse, he's got a gas mask on! This can't be good.

"This won't take long, kid," says Nuclear Disaster Man, coming at me with a strip of something wiggly and flesh-colored. "By the time I'm through, even your grandmother won't recognize you."

I instinctively back away, but there's nowhere to go. "No. Seriously. Don't do that."

He laughs and presses the leechy thing on my nose. "Don't worry, I'm kidding. The captain told me to go easy." Then he smoothes another one on my chin and starts massaging me with a tiny brush like I'm a Play-Doh project.

I'm about to scream that I can't take it anymore when ND Man steps back to assess his work, my face. He turns to his cart and starts ferreting through his drawers until he finds what he's looking for. With a satisfied grunt, he rips the mask off his head and grins. "The final touch," he says, fitting a pair of Harry Potter spectacles over my eyes.

Then he whips off my cape and holds up a mirror.

Well, well... the odds are getting better; we might just pull off this little masquerade.

CHAPTER SEVENTEEN

Agent Moxie shows up with a thick folder of papers and looks me up and down. "Nice work," she calls over to the reconstruction team. They are working frantically to put the finishing touches on Gran, who, for the record, no longer looks anything like my grandmother.

Agent Moxie turns back to me and Captain Thompson, opens the folder and starts the briefing. She's acting like the other day—when I shot her with the sedative stick—never happened.

We cover everything from the layout of the mall to my new "pen." And the small fact that, as of this moment, I'm supposed to answer to the name Finn. The captain jokes that they threw darts to decide what to call me, but even though I didn't choose it—again—I think it's a cool name. Definitely better than Billy.

It takes them a few minutes to go over the entire plan and make sure I have everything I need. They even upgraded my SpiPod to a SpiPhone and showed me how to use it. Not that I'll be making any calls on it, but my equipment is getting better; now I have satellite radio. By the time they're finished, Gran is, too, and she springs out of her chair, decked out as the "fabulously rich" Ina Klum.

She comes straight for me and dusts off my freshly steamed

suit. Then she adjusts her glasses and leans in to give my new spiked hair and reshaped face a hard look. She nods and sends an appreciative glance to my architects. "Superb job, even off-site," she says. "What do you think, Clayton? Or should I say Finn?"

She's right. And I think the biggest difference is my hair. Even though the rest of me has only been "tweaked," it would take my best friend to recognize me.

Outside the double doors, a jet-black vehicle that looks like a pimped-out golf cart is waiting. It's completely enclosed, and I follow Gran and Captain Thompson inside it. The driver's spot is partitioned so that we have our own private compartment, where a lady in a navy-blue pantsuit is waiting for us. She introduces herself as Adelaide Wynn, Senator Meldon's assistant, and as the fancy wheels get going she tells us what to expect at the press conference.

"You'll enter the hangar through a back entrance. Your plane arrived a few minutes ago"—she gestures somewhere ahead of us—"and we've directed the media to a private room for the conference. Local news affiliates and publications only, but they've been given your afternoon's agenda, and in return for the information we've fed them, they have agreed to leave you alone when you shop and visit museums." She hesitates and glances at the notebook in her lap before continuing. "Keep in mind, nobody knows the senator's wife and daughter are missing. We've worked very hard to keep it quiet.

"The senator is inside," she says, nodding toward a door. "I should warn you, he's probably quite a mess at this point."

She consults her notebook again, and in the space of one second, Gran gives the captain a severe expression and Captain Thompson glares right back at her. They've both turned blank faces to Ms. Wynn by the time she looks up.

Okay, that was weird.

We all step out of the golf cart and follow Ms. Wynn through the door and into a small office, where Senator Meldon is pacing as he waits.

Gran shakes his hand and simultaneously pulls me forward. I stick out mine, since the senator seems to be expecting it. He's shorter than he looks on television. And his Clorox smile is kind of ridiculous against his tanned skin. He doesn't seem like a mess to me.

Before any of us can say a word, Ms. Wynn hurries us through the next door. On the other side, it's a crowd of glaring flashes and cameras and bobbing heads, all trying to get a closer look at us. I'm suddenly thankful for my disguise, because it's almost like a coat of armor—and I need it.

I look back at the senator and a charge of guilt runs down my gut. Maybe his teeth and his tan are *his* armor. 'Cause it must be tough to stand in front of these reporters all the time, especially now, when he's so upset about his wife and daughter and can't let on to anybody.

Gran's hand is still on my shoulder as she plants me in front of some dark-blue drapes. A minute later Gran and the senator are sitting at a linen-covered table lined with glasses of water and poofy microphones, facing a room full of reporters who are chattering, waiting for the conference to begin. Ms. Wynn is standing at a podium to the side, and I'm a yard or two behind Gran and the senator, wondering what I'm supposed to do.

Ms. Wynn blows into a microphone to make sure it's working. "If everyone could get settled, we need to get started. Senator Meldon, Mrs. Klum, are you ready?"

A burst of energy surges through the room as hands fly up. Ms. Wynn points to a man wearing an oxford shirt and khakis, who stands and looks directly at Gran. "Mrs. Klum, can you please tell us if your visit is primarily to support the senator in his reelection campaign?"

Gran gives her microphone a quick tap and speaks slowly and carefully, in a clipped accent I've never heard before. "I support any member of our government who sees the advantages of using clean resources, like the wind, to harness energy. This is true clean energy. So, I fully support Senator Meldon and the rest of the Clean Energy Committee." Gran pauses for a moment before adding with a chuckle, "Of course, my grandson, Finn, and I are going to take full advantage of the shopping. North Dakota is a beautiful state to live in, but there's room for improvement where department stores are concerned."

The room breaks out in laughter and Gran and Senator Meldon lock eyes and the senator sends her a brief, appreciative nod. I guess she nailed it. The back-and-forth between Gran and the senator and the reporters continues for a few more minutes and then Ms. Wynn says, "We have time for one more question." She points to a woman in the front row who's wearing a royal-blue sweater with a red scarf around her neck and is sitting at the edge of her seat. The woman stands up and her eyes land on me. Me? What'd I do?

"My question is for Mrs. Klum's grandson. So, Finn, are you game for all this shopping your grandmother has planned?"

I don't know what else to do, so I step forward as Gran makes room for me between her and the senator, and I lean down to Gran's mic.

"Uh, yes. I'm very excited to spend hours and hours following my grandmother around shopping malls." I start to stand straight again, but then something comes to me and I lean back to the mic. "Can somebody tell me where the nearest Best Buy is?"

Everybody laughs, but the woman's not finished. "Hasn't anyone warned you about the mall napper?"

Except for the warning bells I hear going off in my brain, the room is silent. I open my mouth to say something, but the senator reaches over Gran and pats me on the back and answers for me. "The shopping malls are quite safe—our local authorities are working with a number of federal agencies and will have that situation well in hand very soon."

Ms. Wynn interrupts before the senator can respond further. "That's all for today. Thank you very much for coming," she says in a firm voice. And then we're ushered out of the room, which is suddenly abuzz with energy that has nothing to do with windmills.

In the back office the senator pulls Gran aside to say good-bye. He kisses her cheek and then whispers something in her ear.

Captain Thompson is in the corner talking on his cell phone, so I stand where I am and wait for somebody to tell me what to do. Ms. Wynn seems to have the same problem I do, and she smiles at me. "You did a great job in there, Clayton," she says. Then she steps closer and I instantly feel better, not so alone. "I want to tell you good luck today. I don't know Mrs. Meldon very well, but I spend a lot of time getting Amber back and forth from her gym." Then her eyes light up and she catches her breath. "You know, Amber loves your diner, Big Stone's. We're always picking up to-go orders for her, since her parents are so busy—it's her absolute favorite restaurant."

"Really? That's nice. Gran will like to hear that."

Ms. Wynn nods, smiling. "Her favorite is the fried chicken with hot sauce. And she always orders a bucket of sauce, not those little packets. *They* drive her crazy. She dips her chicken straight into the bucket so it's dripping." She shudders at the thought of it. "Oh, and the three-berry pie, of course. We both love that."

That's one of my favorites, too. "Do you order it warm?"

Her mouth opens into a perfect O, like she never thought of that. "They'll warm the pie for us?"

I laugh, because at that moment, Ms. Wynn doesn't seem like a senator's big-time assistant. "Oh, yeah, and they'll send ice cream, too. That's the way I get it."

"Clayton, I'm glad I talked to you." She reaches out and squeezes my shoulder. "I'll be crossing my fingers for you today. I'm really worried about Amber; she's a special girl. Stay safe." Her expression is grim as she backs away and follows her boss, who's walking out the door, talking into his cell phone.

Even though I've known about Amber this whole time, something in the way Ms. Wynn talked about her makes me think. What if Amber and her mom never make it home? Whatever happens to them, good or bad, has a lot to do with me.

I start toward Gran, but now she's on her phone, too. Her lips are pulled in tight, and when I hear her snap at the person on the other end of the conversation to "get busy, then!" I know she's not happy. Now is not the time to share my fears.

Next thing I know, we're back in the golf cart with Captain Thompson and nobody's saying a word.

Something is not right. I can feel it.

Captain Thompson finally speaks. "The senator wants to stick with the plan, doesn't he?"

Gran considers this with a grimace. "So far, yes. But we must move fast—before one of those reporters realizes his wife and daughter are missing—and it's connected to the mall napper problem."

"He's thinking about going public?"

"Not yet," says Gran. "But with each hour that passes, we do have to reevaluate, Derek, you know that." The golf cart comes to a stop and she turns to face the captain. "We've discussed this before, and I understand that the president's friendship with the senator is coming into play, but we really must take another look at the senator and any other family members. It's standard protocol in these types of situations."

"Chief, you know how those kinds of questions can backfire. The president will get involved, and then—"

"I know. It puts us in a very difficult position. But it's as much to protect the senator as anything else." Gran scoots across the seat. "Clayton, it's time."

We both get out, leaving Captain Thompson alone. He sticks his head out and says, "I'll be set by the time you get to the mall. All eyes will be on you two."

And then he's speeding away.

"Gran, what were you saying about the senator and—"

She shakes her head. "Nothing, Clayton. It's just difficult to ask the tough questions when powerful people are involved. Right now we must focus on our job, which is to lure in the bad guys. We have to find Amber and her mother before anything terrible happens to them."

"But what if—"

She holds up her hand. "There is no 'what if.' 'What if' is for planning strategy. Now it's 'what *is*.' We react to what *is*, Clayton. Do you understand the difference?"

"Pretty much."

"Good," she says.

Thirty seconds later, we're walking through the VIP parking area. Nobody notices at first, but I see them. Photographers, news crews, people with microphones ready to go, all standing around waiting. It's not until Gran hands the valet her voucher that they wake up, a slow clamor at first, but an instant later the lights are on and they feast like piranhas on a chicken bone. We can hardly move through the tightening swarm.

A Porsche Cayenne, the turbo version, is waiting, and the valet is trying to help us get to it. He's yelling at the reporters, who are shouting things at us, but we ignore them and keep swimming toward the SUV.

Once we're in the car, Gran steers slowly away from the crowd. "If I run over somebody's foot, it's their own fault," she says. Cameras flash, and I wish our windows were blacked out.

I watch the mob dissipate behind us. Their job is done, and we're free to shop.

"All right, Derek, we're on our way to Rich Hill Mall. I don't see any tails, so I think we're clear. Have you spoken with our contact to make sure the footage is online?" She pauses and then says, "Yes, definitely Twitter. And make sure there are photos. Okay. We'll park as planned and head into Neiman Marcus."

About ten minutes later, Gran pulls into the shopping center and heads to the north end of the mall. She turns into the garage and takes us pretty far, where the concrete columns can barely be seen in the dim light. She parks and takes the keys out of the ignition, and puts her hand over mine. "Clayton, this is it. Together we are going to end this."

She sounds so confident that, for a second, I actually believe it's all going to happen exactly the way we've planned. But then I think about everything that's ever happened to me: my parents, Gramps, surprises on the lacrosse field.

Nothing ever turns out the way I expect.

CHAPTER EIGHTEEN

Even though we go straight into Neiman Marcus, my salivary glands react the minute my feet touch the marble floors. There's food in this mall, and my stomach knows it.

Gran gives me one of those accusing looks that make me think she can read my mind. "Finn, why aren't you listening to your iPod?"

"Thanks, Gran," I say, and twist the hanging bud into my ear. "I wouldn't want to miss Captain T's trombone solo."

"Thank you, Clayton," says the captain. "We've got three malls tightly covered right now—and if our information is right, two have perps in place. We want them to choose you and the chief at Rich Hill. If they've been watching the senator as closely as we think they have been, they know Ina Klum and her grandson are at one of their malls. We've done our best to make you very visible, and if they have a ringleader at home feeding them information, I don't know how they can ignore you. You fit their M.O. to a T. Let's hope they go for the big payoff."

Gran cuts in as she steers me to the store's mall entrance. "How many are you watching here?"

"One so far. He's been moving fast, probably getting the lay of the land," the captain answers. "I'd head to the food court—he hasn't been there yet."

"We're here to shop, but I suppose we have time for a sandwich." Gran grins. "Are you hungry, Finn?"

Holy mother of footlongs, the answer to my prayers.

"Are you kidding? I'm always hungry."

We head to the food court, a place I know almost as well as the diner, and I lead Gran straight to Sam's Deli. They make the most delicious Italian subs ever.

I place my order and watch the guy slice the long, fresh-baked roll, swipe spicy mustard on one side and mayonnaise on the other, then stack salami, mortadella, bologna and provolone—layer after layer. I hold my hand up when he starts piling on the veggies. For sure, hold the pickles. With a final drizzle of Italian dressing, he wraps it.

I turn to Gran, who's shuffling a three-inch stack of hundreds and fifties like it's a deck of cards. Talk about making yourself visible.

"Finn," she says loudly, "I thought I had some smaller bills."

I feel like a spotlight is shining on us. "Use a fifty, Gran. We can get change later, okay?"

Gran smiles and hands a bill to the openmouthed girl at the register, who takes it without shifting her gaze from the wad of money. Probably more cash than she's ever seen in her life. It's the most money I've ever seen, too, so I don't blame her.

"Uh, I'm going to find a table," I say, figuring Gran knows what she's doing.

By the time my sub is half eaten, Gran has finished stuffing her bills back into her wallet and is heading my way.

"Finn," she says as her gaze quickly flits across the surrounding tables, "what shall we shop for?"

I shrug. I don't "shop" much. "What about video games?" I say hopefully.

She frowns her answer and reaches across the table for one of my chips.

"You asked," I say, and take a long drink of Coke. "Um, I haven't heard anything in a while. Do you think our equipment's working?"

"*Finn*, please finish and let's get moving."

"I don't know, Gran, I haven't heard anything since..." I tap on my earbud, then on my SpiPhone. Nothing.

I open my mouth to speak, but Captain Thompson's voice bellows in my ear. "Clayton! Your grandmother is trying to tell you to forget about us and act like a kid—we're busy on this side of things, so"—Gran's glaring in her most professional way while the captain finishes—"you have got to learn to keep your mouth shut—understand, Clayton?"

"Finn."

I know he's about to jump through the tiny speaker in my ear. *"What?"*

"My name is Finn, remember? How do you expect me to act like a Finn when you keep calling me Clayton?"

Gran reaches across the table, and to anyone watching it might look like she's rooting through my chips, deciding which one to steal, but she's actually stabbing the inside of my hand with her sharpened fingernail, painted, coincidentally, the color of blood.

"My dear grandson," she says, and her voice is soft and loving, but with every syllable she digs deeper into my skin. "We have a job to do, so please do your employer the courtesy of following orders without questions."

I get it.

"Clayton?"

Gran and I lock eyes and freeze. The voice is horrifically familiar, and I'm afraid to look up. How did she recognize me? I mean, I'm still wearing some version of a Masters monkey suit, but I've got the wig on and my face has been...I feel a burn rush into my cheeks. The captain and Gran were right—I should have been more than "tweaked."

I break away from Gran's intense gaze and look up, straight into the eyes of Laci Peters.

She does a double take, as if now that she's seen me close up she's uncertain. I'm wondering if I should pretend she's got me confused with someone else, when she starts talking. "I thought it was you coming out of Neiman's. I can spot you anywhere by the way you walk. But, wow." She eyeballs every inch of me, like she's examining one of her famous science experiments. "Are you in a play or something? Those glasses, and your hair, make you look, ah, really different."

I tighten my tie without knowing why. I mean, I'm choking enough, aren't I? "Uh, sort of—grabbing something to eat right now. What about you?"

"Don't you remember?" Laci scrunches her eyebrows together like she's disappointed.

Remember? What am I supposed to remember? And then I see it across the food court. Pretzel Power. Oh, crud. "You're here to order pretzels for..."

Laci throws her teeth on high beam and nods like a bobble-head doll. "Yes! For the meeting tomorrow morning. You're coming, aren't you?" She looks at Gran, then back at me, pulls out a chair and sits, leaning real close. "I nominated you. If we team up we can be president and vice-president together. You're the only one who can take the jock vote away from Brenda Bickley; she's so difficult to work with. What do you say, Clayton?"

I say she better not use my real name again or Gran's head is going to detonate. Whatever I have to do to get her the heck out of here, I will. "Okay, Laci. Can we talk about it at the meeting, er, tomorrow morning?"

She gets up, satisfied. "Great. I better go. I'm here with my mom, and after we order the pretzels I need a few leotards for gymnastics."

I think we're safe, she's about to go, when she sticks out her hand to Gran. "I'm Laci, by the way. Clayton and I go to school together. Are you Clayton's grandmother?"

Gran's mouth tightens. "Yes, dear, I am."

Laci turns back to me. "Hey, there's a big gymnastics meet this weekend. You two should come. It's at Crow's, right across from Big Stone's. You're there a lot on Saturdays, aren't you, Clayton?"

What? Has she been spying on me? I look at Gran. There's enough voltage in her eyes to catapult Laci clear across the food court in a floor routine nobody but a Special Service agent could imagine.

Gran's voice is polite, with a commanding military edge. "You let us know when your first event is and we'll run right over, won't we? Now, I think you said your mother was waiting?"

I clear my throat and meet Laci's eyes. If she *is* smart, she'll figure out that was a dismissal. Captain Thompson's not saying one word, but I bet he's furious.

Laci steps back, grinning so wide it has to be killing her cheeks. "Okay. Bye, Clayton. It was nice to meet you, Mrs. Stone."

"Likewise." The word is dripping sugar, laced with a heavy dose of arsenic.

Laci walks away, the pleats of her navy-blue skirt swinging back and forth with each step, and I feel very sorry for Toby. That girl is going to be trouble for him. For anybody.

"Finn?"

I face Gran—she's looking at me, and everywhere else, too. I take the last bite of my sub and mumble something even I can't understand.

"Your friend Laci is very sharp."

What does she want me to say? I swallow. "Yeah, she's probably the smartest kid at school."

"That's not what I mean," says Gran, eyes back on the food court. It's too quiet over the wire. And I feel all the awful things Gran and the captain *aren't* saying to me. Heck, how did they expect me to get rid of Laci, shoot her with my stun pen?

Without warning, Gran stands and grabs my tray. "I think I need a pair of shoes, Finn. And then perhaps we'll go to the electronics store. We're supposed to be filling shopping bags, after all."

I follow her. All over the mall. For forty-five minutes she takes every opportunity to flash her cash. And I collect her bags, one at a time, while keeping an eye on every single man we pass, imagining he's got a gun hidden inside his jacket. I even scrutinize the mall cop. Is he really a mall cop? *That* would be a good cover.

I hear background noise from the captain and his people, but not much is going on. The guy they thought was casing the place for potential victims got in his car and drove away, alone. It's looking better and better. If the captain doesn't change the plan, I might just make it to my game.

None of the shopping bags are heavy, and I guess Gran planned it that way. It's all part of the act.

"We've got something happening, the cameras have picked up..." The captain's voice is tentative, and his tone makes both Gran and me slow way down.

"Which way?" murmurs Gran.

"Head to the south entrance. No, wait. Sorry. The feed keeps blacking out. He's by Macy's. Go to Macy's and I'll...he must have been staked out right outside the camera's view. I had Agent Moxie move the Porsche to the west garage so it's more central. I've got two agents trying to find his partner right now, but I'm pulling them."

I don't look at Gran, but I have to ask. "That's completely on the other side of the mall. Is he sure?"

"Something must have added up. Walk fast, Finn, this is going to happen quickly. I can feel it."

The captain's voice cuts in again. "Okay, go directly to the Macy's west entrance. The Porsche is in the west parking garage. Center aisle, all the way back. Follow your grandmother's lead, Clayton. Remember, we need him to take you to wherever they're holding Amber and her mom."

Gran wraps her arm around me. "I love you, sweetheart. Stick close to me and remember, you have your pen."

I rub my hand over the pocket of my dress blues and feel the outline of my weapon. It might not be a gun, but like the sedative stick, if it works, it'll be all I need.

We hustle down the marble floors of the department store toward the west entrance. The store is practically deserted, only the salespeople in sight. I have my pen, and I know Gran's got to be fully loaded. Besides, nothing's going to happen until we get to the SUV.

We push through the glass doors and a strong breeze hits my face. And I can't help it, my gaze shifts left, even though the captain's gonna yell at me since that's where the napper might be. But there's nobody. Nothing but an enormous clay planter. My eyes are drawn to the ground next to the planter and my brain begins to tick off details, everything the captain's told me over the past couple of days. What I see begins to register just when the captain shouts in my ear, "Clayton, get inside the mall. Now!" and Gran squeezes my arm and starts pushing me back to the glass doors.

But I can't turn away from the pile of peanut shells on the ground beside the planter. He was here. Was. And the realization shuts down my heart like a busted assembly line.

"Chief, secure yourselves in the mall. The cameras are blind again, but the last feed had him closing on two females south of you. We've got agents scrambling, but—"

Everything the captain is saying is like a jigsaw puzzle coming together. The guy was right there. Waiting. We're too late. He's gone after somebody else. Two females. Agents are on their way. But...but what? Two females. Something strange about the way those words came out of the captain's mouth. Something is wrong. What?

"Yes, I know," says the captain's impatient voice, answering someone I can't hear. Then he talks to Gran. "Chief, take his earpiece—it's a known civilian."

My mouth drops open as Gran rips the wires from my ears, dislodging my SpiPhone and sending it to the ground. "Gran? What's going on?"

"Go!" she says, jerking the entrance door open and shoving me through it at the same time.

I stiffen. My heart may have stopped working, but my body hasn't. I'm not going anywhere until she explains. "What is it?"

Gran looks toward the south parking garage, and that's when the final piece of the puzzle fits into place. There can be only one reason they don't want me to see—or hear—what's going on. A "known" civilian. Oh, no. And the agents; they're "scrambling," but can they get there in time?

I shut my eyes for a split second. There's no time to think, I have to act.

Now.

CHAPTER NINETEEN

My grandmother's grip tightens. "Don't—"

But in a swift motion, I buck her hold and run. We're *not* going to lose this guy. We're not going to lose—

The clack of her heels sounds immediately at my back as I leap off the oversized curb onto the street and follow the deepening slope of the road, cringing at the thought of Gran covering the same ground. Still running, I turn back to see her land, a perfect ten, on the asphalt. There's a triumphant, determined look in her eyes that is very familiar, and I know for a fact that she won't stop until she catches me.

She shoots out of her landing like a gymnast getting ready to vault. But a gymnast doesn't wear designer shoes, and when Gran pushes off, one of her perfectly coordinated heels snaps.

I circle back, but there's nothing I can do as her leg flies to the sky and the rest of her drops like lead and lands in a crumple on the blacktop. For a split second I hesitate, and she screeches at me with pained determination. "Clayton Stone, you listen to me. There is nothing you can do except stay out of the way. Let them do *their* job."

In that instant I know it's not true. I'm not just a decoy. I'm part of the team that has to catch this gang of nappers. And I have to try.

I fling my fake glasses behind me and kick my legs into fifth gear. No stick, no ball, but I'm darn sure heading for a goal. Laci and her mother.

The parking garage in front of me is on the south side of the mall, with outdoor parking lots on either side. The whole place is landscaped like a friggin' botanical garden, and there are trees and bushes and enormous pots of flowers: plenty of places to hide.

I slow to a jog as I approach the wide-mouthed entrance, my eyes stumbling over every stop sign, every faraway head bobbing out of view.

What am I looking for? What are the Special Service agents looking for? They don't know. *Nobody*, not even the captain, knows what kind of vehicle they're searching for. I might not like Laci, but I see her get out of her mom's car every day before school.

"Captain," I say to my wig, my jacket, my shoes, whatever. "Laci's mom drives a dark-blue Volvo, one of those crossovers."

I turn to the row on my left and eliminate parked cars with a rapid, methodical eye. Then, starting at the top of the ramp leading up to the second level, I check off every single car within view. Lots of blue. No Volvos.

It has to be parked on this level, otherwise Laci and her mom would have gone out another way. But where? Maybe one of the outside lots?

I stare straight ahead—it's a long way down in the dark.

Then something cracks on the concrete, like a dropped cell phone. I peer down into the deep, shadowy place where the sound came from, looking and listening. I'm not sure what I'm waiting for, until I hear the next familiar noise. The abrupt catch of a car door.

I want to move, to run to the car that's buried between the other, bigger SUVs somewhere in the rows of concrete pillars, because I know, without even seeing, it's the Volvo. But I stand, paralyzed. There's something else in the air and it's gripping me even tighter than the sounds I heard. Fear.

I force my feet to stutter forward. "Captain, I'm pretty sure I know where Laci and her mom are. If I'm right, our perp has them and is about to leave the south garage. Get your cars ready."

It's like I'm walking toward a tidal wave that's threatening to crash, but it's not hovering over me. It's over Laci. And her mom. And that's what keeps me moving. Laci doesn't have a sedative stick. Her mother doesn't have a gun. They didn't know the danger they'd face when they came to this mall, or the madman they'd encounter. Heck, she wouldn't have even come to the mall today if it weren't for me.

White lights flicker and the Volvo backs out of its space. I take a deep breath. There's only one way to handle this. "Captain, don't stop me," I whisper to my blazer.

The Volvo inches forward, its wheels rolling slowly toward the exit. I try really hard to imagine that I'm catching up with Laci, looking for a ride home.

I shape my mouth into a smile and wave, keeping a steady stride across the concrete until I'm standing directly in front of the vehicle. I stand firm, waving and smiling until the Volvo is forced to stop—or hit me.

I look through the windshield into Laci's mother's panicked eyes. Her lips move only slightly, but she's clearly warning me away.

A few days ago I felt the same desperation. I take another deep breath and dismiss the memory. Right now there's enough to worry about—the tiny hairs, shocked stiff and electrifying the length of my body, are proof of that.

"Hi!" I shout, moving around to the passenger side of the vehicle. The garage is dark, and the Volvo's tinted windows make it impossible to see anyone in the backseat. I pray Laci's mom will lower the window. She does.

"My grandmother had to go somewhere, and I was wondering if you could give me a ride?" I grip the door handle and pull up slightly. It's locked. I look at the driver's-side controls and hope I only have to use one move to get into the car.

"Uh, sweetie, now is not a good time. We have to get Laci to gymnastics, and we're late."

It's really nice of Laci's mom to not want to give me a ride. And I hate to be pushy, especially when she's being so nice in such a not-nice way. But this is my job.

I reach inside and flip the plastic lever, hoping I get it right. The lock pops and I flick the handle, open the door and hop into the front seat, shutting the door behind me. "No problem. I can go to the gym with you. Big Stone's is right across the street, anyway."

Laci's mom doesn't say anything, she just sort of sighs.

"Clayton." It's Laci, but her voice is thin and scared—unrecognizable compared to her usual power-chick self. I know that once I turn around, I'm in this for good.

I rub my pocket and remind myself of two things. First, the captain can probably hear everything that's going on, and second, I have a weapon. It won't kill, but it will stun the heck out of this guy, and that's very good, except—

I turn around and see the guy for the first time. He has a gun aimed right at Laci. And that gun *will* kill.

A shot of fear fires like an asteroid through my veins, but then I look closer, and for a second my brain is confused. The guy can't be very old. Maybe twenty. He's wearing a cutoff T-shirt and jean shorts. I follow his arm to where it bends like a boomerang around Laci's tiny body, all the way to where the gun is mashed against her neck.

"Hey," I say to the guy. It doesn't come off as casually as I mean it to, but there aren't any do-overs, so I have to keep going. I shift my gaze to Laci, wedged inside the crook of his arm. Her eyes scream a desperate plea, and I know she's terrified. I must help her. This time, I want to help her.

"So, are you Laci's gymnastics coach? I heard you were tough on her, but this is overkill, don't you think?"

"Turn around, kid. Lady, why'd you have to pick him up?" He mutters to himself, then kicks the seat. "I don't have time for this. Just drive."

I've gotta stay cool, like the captain would, or Gramps. So I face front and think about what to do next.

Laci's mom's hands shake as she follows the guy's terse directions. Right. Left. Left. Right. She turns the car as he orders, this way, then that, unwiped tears streaming down her face as she drives and sniffs.

I want to comfort her, but that would be a waste of time. I've got to get us out of this car. I face front and stick my hand in my pocket. The guy obviously has his mind made up about how this is going to go down, and I finger the smooth metal pen. I have to be ready. Didn't Gran say the thing could fire through stuff? Maybe not upholstered leather, but dress pants? Sure. If he'd only move away from Laci.

The question is not what I'll do, but when. Backup's got to be close by now. Maybe the captain's waiting to see if he'll take us to the hideout. If only I had my SpiPhone. It's one thing for Gran and me to let them kidnap us, but I don't think Laci and her mom should have to risk their lives. This is all messed up.

I've got to let the captain know where we are. I look out the window for a way to tell him. "Uh, are we headed out of town? I know that place—Luby's. We eat breakfast there sometimes when Gran's sick of the diner."

A hard knock shakes my seat. "What's wrong with you, kid? You need to shut up!"

The guy has moved. He's gotten angry and moved, I'm sure of it. Away from Laci? Did he kick my seat with his foot, or whack it with his gun?

There's only one way to find out. I turn and make no secret of scrutinizing the guy, from his curly blond hair to his colorful Nike sneakers, the same way Agent Moxie did to Wacko #1.

In a quick motion, the man plows forward and raises his hand, brandishing his gun like a lasso he's ready to cinch. "What do you think you're doing, kid?" He throws a string of curses at me, but he's completely let go of Laci.

The time is now. This guy is getting too cranky to have a trigger at his fingertips. Keeping my eye on his gun, I forget everything else. I inch my fingers downward and feel the impression of the button I pray will save us.

I aim and squeeze. The pen vibrates in my hand and fires a simultaneous flash that frames Wacko #2 in a crackle of light. One surprised blink and a series of shudders later, he drops his gun and slumps sideways, his eyes rolling backward into their sockets.

The car jerks to a screeching stop and we're still. Laci's mom shrieks something I can't understand, but her meaning is clear. We all scramble out the doors and dodge through two tangling lanes of cars that are trying to avoid crashing into us and the rush of Special Service agents sprinting, weapons drawn, toward the Volvo.

It's all turning out pretty good, considering.

Then I spot Gran and the captain, and the way they're looking at me, maybe pretty good isn't good enough.

CHAPTER TWENTY

I turn, my heart thumping hard and fast, and search across the chaos of agents, confused citizens stuck in their cars and beefy black sedans and SUVs, for another way to go, someone else to talk to. A face-to-face with the captain and Gran, who's hobbling toward me with the help of a cane, is the last thing I want.

On the sidewalk a few feet away, Laci and her mom are hugging, wrapped around each other pretzel-like. I cringe. Bad choice of words.

Laci's head is pressed into her mom's jacket, and she opens her eyes and sees me. Immediately, she lets go of her mom and steps my way, her mother following right behind.

"Clayton," Laci says, her voice still shaky and weak, "you saved us. How did you know? How did you do it?"

I want to disappear, because I can't give her the real answer. If she knew everything, if she knew I could have warned her, what would she say?

Mrs. Peters shakes her head. "Clayton, you—we can't thank you enough." She scans the area and then stares hard at the agents still swarming in and around the Volvo, her brow furrowed. "I don't understand—these officers were right here waiting for us." She meets my eyes and her mouth drops open. "Are you involved with these people, Clayton?"

A hand clamps down on my shoulder. There's only one person, besides Gramps, with a grip like that. "I'm Captain Thompson," he says, offering his other hand to Mrs. Peters. "If you and your daughter don't mind, we'd like to bring you down to our offices so you can formally identify the man who assaulted you. There's also some paperwork."

Laci's mom looks from the captain to me to Laci. "Sweetheart, I think you're going to miss practice today."

Laci smiles, but it's only a fraction of her usual smile. The napper didn't take her life, but he did take something. "Yeah," she says, her voice steadier now, "I don't think I'm up to back handsprings, anyway."

Captain Thompson points to a car where an agent is holding a door open. "We'll meet you there," he says to the Peterses, squeezing my shoulder even tighter. I guess I know which car I'm riding in.

Minutes later we're in the captain's black Suburban. Gran is in the front, staring out the windshield, her cane braced between the two front seats. She hasn't said a word, but she doesn't need to. She's mad as heck at me for leaving her. I get it.

The captain sits beside me in the second row and briefly looks at his watch, reminding me of the time. I don't want to bring it up, but is there? Time, I mean?

"Clayton, you broke rank. Your orders from the chief and me were clear. What do you have to say for yourself?"

I feel bad about Gran getting hurt, but everything turned out okay. We rescued Laci and her mom and got another napper off the street, and maybe this one will talk.

The important thing is, all the good guys are still alive. Laci, her mom, me, Gran and all the agents. I turn to Captain Thompson. "I'm sorry. I knew it was Laci and I had to make a choice. Gran had at least two guns and a knife and probably some sort of nuclear device in her purse, so I figured she'd be okay. But Laci and her mom . . ." I pause briefly before I can continue. "Captain, I had to help them if I could."

He grunts. "You lost your earpiece, and your phone." He holds up the SpiPhone, waving it so I'll notice the cracked screen. "How were we supposed to—"

I shake my head and interrupt him. "That wasn't my fault. Gran yanked the cord out of my ear."

"Whatever the reason, you didn't know what was going on, where we were or how to proceed to help the operation."

My arms fly into the air. "I didn't last time, either, remember? Come on, Captain, you needed somebody in the car. The guy had a gun to Laci's neck. What, you think one of your agents was going to walk right up to the car and get in like I did?"

The captain exhales long and loud. "Clayton, to be honest, your grandmother and I don't know whether to fire you or give you a medal."

Huh. Well, I guess that's more like it. "You know, it could have turned out a whole lot worse."

Gran shifts in her seat to face me. Then she turns to the captain. "You know who used to say that?"

Captain Thompson nods back at her and cocks his head my way. "Sometimes it's like he's still here."

Yeah. I wish.

When we get to Special Service headquarters, there are suits everywhere. Suits at computers and on telephones. Suits working up lab requests and transporting bagged evidence. Suits ordering sandwiches and making coffee.

I look at the line of clocks and find one set to Eastern Daylight Time. It's five thirty. And the captain promised, no matter what he has to do, he's going to get me to the field for warm-ups at six thirty.

Special Service agents are questioning the napper, trying to get him to cooperate. But they've decided to turn him over to the local police because some reporter got wind of the arrest. That's not a surprise, since so many people witnessed it, but I can tell Gran and the captain are worried. Gran keeps getting phone calls from the senator—*he's* really worried. The kidnappers are threatening to kill Amber and her mom if the police get involved. The captain says he needs to be worried for another reason: too much time is passing.

But right now there's a game to think about; time to get psyched. I catch a look at myself in one of the glass doorways, and it kinda creeps me out. This getup has got to go. I need someplace to turn "Finn" back into Clayton.

Three hallways branch off the bustling Special Service offices; two of them are lined with doors on either side. I choose the hallway on the left and start down the long corridor, tapping each door as I pass. The hall shifts to the right and then veers off in two directions. If I go much farther, I'm gonna get lost. I grab the next door handle—it feels right somehow—and turn it. The room is dark, so I slip in and fumble for a wall switch. There's a large rectangular piece of glass already reflecting some light into the room, and I grin, realizing I'm on the observation side of an observation window. I look closer and my mouth drops open. Laci and her mother are sitting at a table in the other room.

I try not to let the sight of them distract me as I start picking at my nose and cheeks. The dried rubber falls easily to the ground in thin strips, but when I move on to my wig, it's more of a struggle.

I bite down at the searing pain, which is getting worse with every attempt at separating my head from the rock-star hair I thought was awesome two short hours ago. I can't help staring at Laci while I work.

What I see through the glass is not the perfectly ironed, ribbon-in-the-hair, know-it-all, bossy, manipulative girl who runs seventh grade. No. Her dark, wavy hair is disheveled, with tiny curls pasted to the side of her face. Her cheeks, usually flooded with the pink energy of domination, are pale and drained. And her eyes are filled with something I don't recognize.

Determination, maybe? Only not the sort of determination she uses to get elected or organize a bake sale. This is different. More important.

Out of the corner of my eye, I see the captain enter the other room. His voice booms through the speakers in the ceiling above me. "Laci, Mrs. Peters, how are you?" He shakes hands with Mrs. Peters and pats Laci on the shoulder before he sits. "It's been a rough day for you both, and I want you to know, with your help we're going to send this guy to prison, and hopefully track down the rest of his friends."

"Of course we'll help," says Mrs. Peters. "You won't let him go? I mean, on bail?"

The captain smiles reassuringly. "We've got a lot of evidence—and if any of it matches up, he's not going anywhere. Don't worry." He pauses and leans in, close to Laci. "There's something else we need to discuss. How well do you know Clayton Stone?"

Laci gives him a small smile. "I've gone to school with Clayton since kindergarten—he's like the class clown and a huge jock."

"So, you're friends."

Laci is quiet for a few seconds before she answers. "In a way, but not best friends or anything. I'm running for student council president for our middle school, and I wanted him to run for vice-president." She looks away from the captain, into the mirror, and shakes her head. "Actually, after all this, I think maybe he'd be the one who'd make a good president."

The captain follows her gaze to the observation window. He can't know I'm in here, can he? Then he turns back to Laci and clears his throat. "I guess the point is, you know him well enough. And you two went through something very unusual together. Something nobody else, outside of your mother, and everyone here"—he pauses and sweeps his hand through the air—"will ever understand."

Laci's voice is solemn. "You can say that again."

The captain nods. "And that's what I need to speak with you about. There will be media coverage, and sometime in the next few days, your names will likely come out on television and in the papers. Reporters will want to talk with you. But we don't want anyone to find out Clayton was involved."

Mrs. Peters frowns. "Is that feasible?"

"I don't know, but I hope so. As you may have suspected, Clayton has a relationship with the Special Service, and he sort of stands out because he's—"

"Because he's a kid." Laci finishes the captain's sentence. She stares at him and her eyes grow wide as she begins to understand. Completely understand. "He works for you, and you don't want anyone at school to know, or my dad, or anybody?"

Captain Thompson pulls in his lips. "This case isn't over. In fact, it's getting even more complicated. If word, or his picture, gets out, we can't use him. And although we've never employed a minor before, in his short time with the Special Service, Clayton's proven himself to be quite adept at this sort of work."

Wow. Quite adept. That sounds good. Note to self: Google *adept*.

Laci leans forward and lowers her voice. "Well, it would be great if he started working on some sort of career path. I was thinking politics, myself. But this might work, too."

There's the Laci I know and avoid. We're in seventh grade. I can do anything I want.

The captain is chuckling; I must have missed something. He gets to his feet and pulls business cards from his pocket, giving one to each of them. "These are my direct numbers—my cell's at the bottom. Plug it into your phones and call me if you need anything." He puts his hand on the doorknob and starts out of the room.

"Okay," says Laci, staring at the card.

I'm wondering if it says *At Your Service* like Gramps's did, when Laci looks up again. "Um, can we see Clayton before we leave?"

The captain stops and glances quickly at the window, then back to Laci. "I'm not sure we have time for that," he says. "I believe he's trying to get to his lacrosse game, and he's already running late. Good-bye, ladies, I'll be in touch." And as he's closing the door behind him, he glances once more toward the mirror and winks.

A weird rush washes down my body. I may not know exactly what career I want, but whatever I do, I'm going to learn how to see through walls. Just like Captain Thompson.

CHAPTER TWENTY-ONE

The soles of my shoes screech into the locker room a few minutes before six thirty. Toby's got my bag and a totally relieved look on his face. Then I take off the baseball cap the captain loaned me.

"What the heck did you do?" Toby says, his eyes round as donuts. He zeroes in on my shiny, blotchy head. It's not bleeding, but it's irritated and sore from all my picking. I grin at his reaction. He's definitely impressed, in a black eye or stitches-in-the-butt kind of way.

I stand up a little straighter and rub my scalp. "I got a haircut and it sucked. So Gran shaved it off for me. What do you think?"

It works. I can tell by the way he's circling and nodding. "Extreme," he says.

I take my bag from him and set it on the wooden bench in front of my locker, with a quick glance at the clock as I start stripping down. Less than five minutes to get my uniform on and get out on the field. Toby yells to Percy and Runner as they're about to exit through the big metal door that leads outside. "Hey, Clayton's late. We need a couple hands."

They instantly drop their bags and move toward us while

Toby unzips my bag and starts lining up my pads and uniform and socks. He throws a cleat each to Percy and Runner. "Loosen them," he says.

The rest of the guys are gathering, urging me to hurry as they inspect my gleaming scalp with surprised murmurs. Then somebody calls out, "Hey, all of us should do it!" and as I pull my jersey over my head, the rest of the team echoes the idea. Who knew shaving my head would be the quickest way to bring the team together again?

We're running out of time, so I clamp down on a feeling that's welling up inside me. This team is the best group of friends I've ever had. How can I let them down?

For now, I squash the horrid reality: if I keep helping the Special Service, there's only one thing to do. Quit lacrosse.

I reach down for my stick and my bag and glance around at the teammates who are risking the wrath of Coach to walk out on the field late with me.

I meet Toby's eyes and then look back to the rest of my buds. "Are you bums finally ready?"

And with good-natured pushes and shoves, we head out the locker room door. Together. We've got a game to win.

Through a stroke of luck that will never occur again, Coach is in a stew with the referee because the second ref hasn't shown up, and we can't start the game until he does. He doesn't even notice us as we slip our bags around the home bench and, in groups of twos and threes, take our end of the field for warm-ups.

The other bench is already crowded with St. Ignatius's gear, and their team is on the turf, whipping balls at each other like it's target practice at a shooting range. Dang. Is it my imagination or are their passes even sharper than last week?

Toby and Percy come up beside me. Toby nudges my shoulder and gestures toward their goalie. He's got two coaches pelting him with balls, and he's getting most of them. I look back to Toby and raise my eyebrows. "We better figure that guy out or it's going to be a long game."

Toby nods and heads with Percy onto the field, holding up his stick for a throw. Most of our guys are already running half-fields or tossing balls. When the second ref shows, Coach heads our way with orders to start a couple of sideline-to-sideline drills.

The stands are starting to fill, and as I look at them, I remember Gran won't show. It makes me kind of sad. She never misses my games. But she's got to lie low in her getup until this whole mall napper thing is over. So the captain is my taxi tonight, but he doesn't want to be noticed, either. He insists he'll see the game just fine from his blacked-out Suburban. Which is probably true, since he had Jones post HD cameras the size of paper clips around the field.

The clock counts down while we warm up, and by the time it's set for the first quarter, my legs are loose and I'm ready to play. So far Coach hasn't said a word to me about missing practice on Sunday. Did Gran talk to him, or something? It's the only explanation. I mean, I don't think she told him what I was really doing, but she probably came up with something.

It turns out I do play. The game begins with the first face-off, and somehow, the quarters tick by. Whistle after whistle. Face-off after face-off. Goal after goal. Toby and I finally get the goalie pegged, but his reactions are wicked fast and he's able to block most of our shots. Only, thanks to the goal god, not so many that we fall behind. Neither team leads by more than two the entire game.

By the end of the fourth quarter, we've come from behind and the score is 12–12. I'm all but destroyed. Percy did something to his knee in the second quarter, so I've been playing midfield, running from one end of the field to the other, non-stop. Every muscle aches, and the ignition has gone out of my run. Not only that, but Coach has been using me for most of the face-offs. I've only won two, and that's making me, and everybody else, edgy. With just over a minute left in the game, this next one counts big-time.

I squat and set my stick beside my opponent's. He's

somebody new, and that's not helping my confidence. St. Ignatius has so much depth on their bench, there's a set of new faces out here every few minutes. It stinks I've got no road map on this guy, but there's not a whole lot I can do about it. So I tell my brain to shut up and focus on what actually happens. Finally, I'm centered and ready to clamp down. I want this ball, and my heart pounds as I wait for the whistle.

It blows, and I manage to cover the ball and rake it to the side, where I pray my wingman, Dion, is ready. He is. Dion scoops it up and loops around, cradling the ball as he runs toward the attackmen, looking for me, or Toby, or somebody to set up with. I feel more than see a guy gunning down the field, and register the number with a bad feeling in the pit of my stomach. It's happening too fast to warn Dion: St. Ignatius's dirtiest player, number three, is coming for him.

I've been there. Desperate to crack the ball out of my opponent's pocket. But not desperate enough to come at him with a cross-check from behind. And that's how number three is moving, both hands set to use his stick to plow over Dion.

I yell a warning to Dion just as they collide and the ball flies into the air. Toby catches it with two Ignatius defensemen on his stick, pounding away, until the ball finally pops loose.

The fight for the ball continues, but everybody's waiting for the ref's call that should obviously come as Dion gets to his feet, limping. The flag flies, the whistle blows and two long seconds later the clock stops—we could have used that time. Now there are only nineteen seconds left to play, but on the plus side, number three is sent to the box for the rest of the game.

On the sidelines, Coach is beet-red and screaming. It's our ball, and he wants us to take it at the whistle. "We're man up! Set up and go—twenty-one! Twenty-one!"

Twenty-one is a play we've practiced but never used in a game. It means I take it straight to the crease when the whistle blows, fake right to Toby, move left and shoot high into the right corner. I'm the feature in this play because I'm a lefty, so that increases my odds of success. But even with that advantage, I can only put it on cage fifty percent of the time.

The whistle blows, and immediately I've got a guy on me, frantically slashing my arm as I cradle the ball. I keep my stick back and low and stay on goal. The clock is fading on this game, and I hear Coach call out the seconds as it runs down. Nine. Eight. Seven. The goalie is ready for me, and I know he's got my number. Whatever I've got planned, he's set to take my shot. Only my shot.

Six. Five. The way is open, like a gift, directly in front of me. I can see it—and in two maneuvers I'll have my slot. I can probably score if I send the ball directly over the goalie's head into the far corner of the net. Probably.

Four. Three. But this has got to be a sure thing. In a split second I see my guys; I see sticks and bodies colliding, every player covered. The goalie's huge net faces me, and I see a pocket up, ready as always. Then Toby's guy lunges toward me, leaving Toby wide open. Big mistake.

Two. I feed the ball to Toby, who seizes it out of the air like it was always supposed to be his.

One. He fires into the net at point-blank range.

Zero.

Final score, 13–12.

My orders are to get my stuff and hightail it to the idling Suburban as soon as the game is over. But that's not exactly realistic. 'Cause first we have to ditch our helmets and gloves and line up and shake hands with the other team. Then there's Coach's talk, and holy mother of long-winded, he has a lot to say tonight. Then I have to get my gear together and walk across the field through patches of parents who all stop me to say congratulations.

I've made it across the track and through the fence gate when a familiar voice sounds from my right. "Clayton!"

It's Laci, racing down the bleacher steps. Huh. After this

afternoon, I would have thought she'd be home—with the doors bolted.

I glance behind me, because I for sure don't want Toby to get the wrong idea. He's still by the team bench with some of the guys, so I wave at Laci as she approaches. "Hey."

She stares at my bald head for a second and something flickers at the corners of her mouth. Laughter? Whatever it is, the expression vanishes when our eyes meet.

"Listen, Clayton," she says, leaning close to me, her voice barely above a whisper. "We didn't really get to talk to you after everything that happened, but my mom and I want to thank you so much." She closes her eyes like she's imagining the ride in the Volvo all over again. "We owe you our lives."

I shake my head. "Laci, it's okay, you don't owe me anything. And you already thanked me."

"I'm going to have to thank you every day for the rest of the year, unless I can figure out a way to repay you," she says. Her voice is evenly pitched, not singsongy like it usually is, and she hasn't flashed her big teeth once.

She holds my gaze for a second before she speaks again. "Are you coming tomorrow morning?"

Tomorrow morning. Tomorrow morning. What is . . . ?

"The student government meeting," she says. And even though she's asking me, I can tell she's trying not to be her typical pushy self. She shrugs. "I'm still bringing pretzels. Uh, actually, my dad's going to get them, 'cause I'm never going into a mall again. Ever."

Yeah, it's getting a little old for me, too. But seriously, I'm wiped. And her meeting is at 7:30 a.m. I look at her and I'm about to tell her I can't make it like I usually do when she asks me to show up for something, when an unfamiliar emotion washes over me. Guilt.

I don't want to. I don't want to. I don't want to. "Well, sure. Maybe."

Her lips curve into a quiet half-smile. "Okay, good. I'll see you tomorrow, then." And next thing I know, she's gone, walking away with her mom, who waves and smiles at me, mouthing the words *Thank you* before they step onto the sidewalk that leads to the parking lot.

I'm not sure why I said I'd go to a stupid student government meeting. I don't want to be vice-president of anything.

She's "sharp." Gran's words, not mine.

She's nice. And definitely pretty. I swat the ridiculous thoughts away as if they're bloodsucking mosquitoes. My brain must have short-circuited for a minute. Or something like that.

I hike my bag over my shoulder with a groan and head for the suburban, and as I do, I notice I'm getting a hard look from the other side of the parking lot. Toby.

I nail my eyes to the pavement, pretending I don't see him, and move like I'm late to dinner. 'Cause I am.

CHAPTER TWENTY-TWO

The next morning, I don't make it to the student government meeting. I know Laci's going to be mad, so the last thing I expect when I walk through the school doors is to see her standing, holding a huge pretzel, in the exact spot where Toby usually waits for me. I scan the tiled atrium. No Toby. This is way weird.

"Are you hungry?" she says, holding out the pretzel as I approach. "It's cinnamon sugar—I saved it for you."

I don't know what else to do, so I put my gear down and take the pretzel, keeping an eye out for my mocha. "Thanks," I say, wondering how she figured out my most absolute favorite pretzel ever. "I kind of overslept."

"It's okay. I thought about it and figured you were tired, after yesterday and the game and everything. But I really want to talk to you about student government."

I take a bite of the pretzel and then pick up my bags. "Listen, Laci," I say, moving toward Mr. Davis's room, "I seriously don't think I'm cut out to be in student government or *anything* like that. Besides, I'm pretty busy."

She nods but doesn't say anything, just keeps walking beside me.

"And if you want to know the truth—" I don't know what the actual truth is, so when Toby bumps me from behind, I'm grateful in a ginormous way. Except for the expression on his face when he notices Laci.

"Here's your coffee, man," he says, not taking his eyes off her.

Laci smiles at Toby. "Nice goal last night, Toby." Then her eyes return to me. "Think about it, okay, Clayton?" She stops and backs down the hall in the opposite direction. "I'll see you guys later."

Toby watches her walk away with a confused smile on his face. "What's all that about?"

"Did I tell you somebody nominated me to run for student government VP next year?"

He shakes his head. "No."

"Well, it was her. She's trying to convince me to run."

Toby's mouth drops open. "You? Why?"

I laugh as we move down the hall and turn the corner. "You might as well tell me, 'cause I have no idea—except she says I can get the jock vote away from Brenda."

An impossible-to-ignore shadow crosses Toby's face. But that's what I do: ignore it. And head a little faster toward Mr. Davis's classroom.

CHAPTER TWENTY-THREE

By the end of the day, I think every single kid at Masters Academy has rubbed my bald head, so I'm not the most hated guy on the team anymore. Only, there are still a few things I have no clue how to handle.

Like the class VP thing. It's bothering me, and I can't figure out why. I mean, it's easy; tell the girl no. But "no" is more complicated now that I helped Laci and her mom out of the situation I got them into in the first place. And now that she doesn't annoy me as much as she used to.

All through the day, I keep seeing Toby's face when he realized she asked me to run—not him.

After school I blow right by the captain's black Suburban, until a loud voice stops me in my tracks. "Hey, Clayton, where're you going?" His big head is sticking out of the truck's rear window.

"Uh, I think I've got a meeting with somebody important, but I can't remember who it is," I say.

He grins, and for once his whole face looks happy, which is weird; he usually doesn't smile for real.

"Get in, Clayton. I've got to fill you in."

I step into the back of the vehicle and sit beside him. "What's up?" I say as the Suburban pulls into traffic and rolls down the busy street. He holds out his hand for my cell phone and gives me what must be a brand-new SpiPhone in return—no cracked screen. It's an exchange I'm getting used to.

"Well," he says, tucking my cell into his jacket, "the dual interrogations haven't gone as planned. If they know where they're keeping Mary Lou and Amber, neither guy is talking."

I stare at him. "Do you think they're alive?"

He shrugs back at me. "I'll tell you what I do know. I know it was at least one member of this gang who took them. But something is bothering me, Clayton."

He's dead silent, and at least a minute goes by before he explains. "You see, the guy we caught yesterday spotted you and your grandmother in the food court. He was there. He saw her flipping through all that cash—more money than they usually pull in from their ATM routine."

This is a shocker. "He did?"

"Yeah." The captain nods. "I wasn't positive, because I was doing surveillance from the monitors in here. I had two agents in a stakeout van, and one of them told me he was sure the same guy tapped you two in the food court. I went back and looked at the tapes, and it *was* him.

"So it dawned on me, why didn't he go for you and your grandmother? You fit all his requirements, woman and kid, obviously wealthy, distracted and shopping."

Huh. Why did he go after Laci and her mom instead? "So what was wrong with us?"

The captain raises his eyebrows and cocks his head, like, *Who knows?*

I'm having trouble putting this together. "They went after the senator's wife and daughter—what was different about them?"

"Maybe it's not what's different. Maybe it's what's the same. The numbers are starting to talk; almost seventy-five percent of the kids have been girls."

So maybe I should tell him. "Laci's a girl."

He doesn't even skip a beat. "Yes, Clayton, I am aware of that. But that can't be all of it. What about the twenty-five percent who were boys?"

I get it. We need to think harder. I look out the window at the muted blur of trees as we speed down the parkway. Something is not making sense. What is it? I look back at him. "Captain, were all the other attacks on people who had money?"

He nods.

"And they all drove nice SUVs? I mean, not just seventy-five percent of them?"

The captain looks at me and then grabs a file folder from the seat pocket in front of him. He starts flipping through pages inside it. Turning back to me, he nods again. "Yes. Definitely. Why?"

"And were the side windows tinted on all of them? I mean"—I tap the blacked-out windows of the Suburban—"not like this, but dark?"

He looks back to the pages on his lap, shaking his head as he reads. "It doesn't say, but we can find out."

"Well, if they are, maybe that's part of what they're looking for, you know, to help them hide. So they pick the mom and kid *before* they go into the mall, after they've seen the car. 'Cause if they're riding around with a gun to a kid's head, they don't want anybody to notice, right?"

The captain sits back in his seat. With a grimace, he taps the darkened glass; a second later he's on the phone. "Look at every single one of the victims' vehicles in the mall napper case. I want to know if they had tinted windows. If they did, how dark, and was it every window, or only the back ones? Yes. Including the senator's—" He pauses. "Yes, I understand it's still missing. How do you think? Call him and ask!"

The captain hangs up and stares at me. "The SUV you and Agent Moxie—"

I wag my head. "Yeah, it had dark windows, but the Porsche from yesterday didn't—plus, you guys moved it, remember?"

"And Laci's car?"

I sigh, because this might really add up. "Dark. Not like yours, but darker than most tinted windows."

Captain Thompson shakes his head, lines of regret forming around his mouth. "Why didn't anybody plot this out?"

But he shouldn't feel bad. He got pulled into this because the president of the United States asked him to help, because of Senator Meldon. "Uh, Captain, it wasn't a Special Service assignment until a few days ago, remember? You can't know everything."

The expression on the captain's face doesn't change, I guess because it doesn't really matter whose fault it is. He feels responsible. He turns back to the manila folder on his lap and speaks in a tight, deep tone. "It's my job to put information together. Complete and fast."

I don't know what else to say. I definitely can't make him feel better. Heck, I feel bad, too. "Where are we going? A different mall?"

"No," he says. "We're meeting your grandmother and the senator at the Marriott over by Key Bridge."

"So we're not going to set up at the malls anymore?"

"Enough with the questions, Clayton. Let's get to the hotel first."

I get it. "You don't know, do you?"

Captain Thompson doesn't answer; he just flips through his huge file for the rest of the ride.

CHAPTER TWENTY-FOUR

When we get to the hotel, we go in through a back door that leads directly into a long hallway. There's an elevator to our immediate right, and the doors slide open like it's been waiting for us; the captain presses button 14 and we ride in silence.

The hotel room is full of suits, most of them on their cell phones or laptops. Gran is sitting in an armchair talking to some-body on her computer; her face and hair are back to normal and there's no sign of her cane. Senator Meldon is on the couch with his assistant, Ms. Wynn, right beside him. She's trying to type every single thing he says on her small tablet. Twice she scoots a half-full glass toward the middle of the table, probably so it won't spill and ruin her keyboard. But each time she moves it, the sena-tor picks it back up, takes a drink and starts talking again.

A man stomps out of one of the bedrooms and closes his eyes in frustration. "No," he groans loudly to the room, "we couldn't trace him. It was a completely different phone number and he turned it off again."

The senator stands up and shakes his head when he hears this. Then he turns back to Ms. Wynn. "Okay," he says. "Where were we?"

Ms. Wynn shoots a nervous look at Captain Thompson, who

goes over and shakes hands with the senator—to distract him? I can't hear what they're saying, but the senator looks directly at me and waves me over as he sits beside Ms. Wynn again. "Clayton," the senator says when I'm standing across from him. "Have a seat."

I catch Gran's eye as I back into the chair beside her. I figure the stern look she's shooting me is a message to remember my manners around such an important person. I want to say "Duh," but that wouldn't be polite.

"Young man, I can't thank you enough for helping us out. I heard you caught two of the suspects practically single-handed. Bravery like that should be rewarded." The senator's voice is booming, like he's giving a speech in the Capitol. He looks around the hotel room, nodding, and I sort of feel like he's not talking to me.

"Uh, well, I wanted to help, you know, so nobody else would get attacked."

The senator laughs, and I wonder why he thinks that's funny. I turn quickly to the captain to see if he's laughing, too. But Captain Thompson is staring at the senator with a troubled expression.

I feel like I'd better keep talking over the weirdness in the room. Is the senator drunk? "I'm sorry we haven't found your family yet."

He waves his hand at me. "Yes. Everyone's doing their best. But you, young man, are a credit to this country. Not like some teenagers I know. Take, take, take. Shop, shop, shop." The senator brings his drink to his lips for another long swallow and then drops the empty glass on the gleaming wood table with a loud clunk. He leans forward and points his finger, first at Gran and then at the captain. "What you have to do is find the ringleader. Because he's never going to be the one who goes to the mall, mark my words. You've got to find him where he lives. He'll keep hiring thugs to work the malls. It's basic business sense. I should know. We must go to the American people. They will help us."

I turn my eyes to the captain, who's slowly nodding his

head. "Rest assured, we're still working on every possible angle, Senator." Then his eyes find me. "Clayton, I think we should be going. Will you please wait in the hall while I talk with your grandmother?"

Gran gets up, puts her arm around my shoulders and whispers in my ear. "I'll see you as soon as we have a plan together. You've been a tremendous help, Clayton, but now it's up to us." She turns to the captain. "Captain Thompson will take you back to headquarters. Do you remember Frankie, my assistant?"

I nod. Sort of. "She got me a Coke the other day?"

"Yes," Gran says. "She'll show you where you can sleep, and she'll get you up in the morning." Taking both my hands, she continues. "I know it's your birthday tomorrow, and that all of this might interfere with our usual celebration."

"No, Gran, don't worry. We can do cake and stuff after this is over."

She squeezes my hands and smiles. "Well, in the morning you'll take the elevator to the diner for breakfast. Carlos has orders to take care of you. And I told him, no pickles! Okay?"

I laugh at that. "Okay."

"Now, please wait in the hallway while I speak with Derek."

"Sure," I say. I haven't had one of Carlos's breakfasts in a while, and the thought of his buttermilk waffles makes me immediately optimistic.

I walk out of the hotel room and close the door behind me. I wonder how they're planning to find the "ringleader" like the senator said. And what did he mean about going to the American people? He's all over the place and so loud and clumsy, he has to be drunk. He must be taking all this pretty hard. Whatever. It doesn't sound like they need me anymore.

A second later the door opens and Ms. Wynn slips into the hallway. She looks up and down the corridor and then takes my arm and walks me down the hall. "Clayton, I'm sorry you've gotten involved in this. It must be very scary for you."

"It's okay. At least we got two of them." Something is wrong.

I can feel it in the urgent way she's squeezing me and practically dragging me away from the hotel room.

She takes a deep breath, like she wants to say something but doesn't know how to start. "Take this," she says, stuffing a piece of paper in my hand as we walk. "Give it to your grandmother as soon as you can get her alone. I've been trying, but it's impossible. Tell her I know the voice we heard earlier on the phone. The napper. Do you understand? The first man who called here today asking for the ransom—they had him on speakerphone and I heard part of the conversation. And I recognized his voice."

I'm confused. If Ms. Wynn recognizes the voice, why is she telling me? "But shouldn't you say something to Gran? Or Captain Thompson? They're sitting right there."

Ms. Wynn shakes her head. "It's really complicated, Clayton. I'm only an assistant—if I tell them about this, I could get fired. Or maybe worse." We've made it all the way down the hall to the elevator, and as she looks back toward the hotel room, she gives my hand with the paper in it a brief squeeze. "Tell her to check the calls made to this phone number. I've spoken to this guy on numerous occasions, before any of this started. All along I thought he was the senator's gardener or something. I tracked him down from the senator's contact list that I keep on my computer. The phone number in your hand is that creep's *personal* number."

She presses the down button with an impatient finger, keeping a close eye behind us as she waits for the elevator doors to open. "That's all I can say. Remember—give it to your grandmother. No one else. She's the only person who has the security clearance to get proof. Tell her: the phone number and the voice. That's all she needs to know, do you understand?"

I try to answer, but I barely manage a nod before her head swings from the elevator that isn't opening to the exit door a few steps away. She darts toward the door like she's being chased, turns the knob and disappears into the stairway. As the heavy door glides shut, I hear her heels clatter down the metal stairs, getting farther and farther away.

The door finally clicks closed, and I turn directly into the curious gaze of Captain Thompson. "I thought you were going to wait for me. Why are you down here?" he says, looking from me to the elevator, whose doors are now wide open.

"I have no idea," I say. And that's the truth.

6:40 p.m.

Frankie hands me a Chipotle bag and a bottle of water and points to the seating area outside Gran's office, where she first brought me a Coke. I sit and proceed to inhale the overstuffed burrito, salad and chips with guac and salsa until I'm stuffed.

I'm tired and about to drop my head on the couch for a snooze when Frankie appears through a doorway and swipes a card across one of the picture frames down the hall from Gran's office. The wall slides open, and she turns and signals for me to follow. "It's getting late, Clayton, so we better get you settled."

At this point nothing should surprise me, but my mouth drops open anyway as she shows me around the hidden apartment. "This comes in handy sometimes," she says. "There are two bed-rooms, three baths, a media room and a kitchen, which is not stocked at the moment." After the three-minute tour, she leaves me in my bedroom with orders to do my homework and get to sleep. She points down the hall as she leaves and says, "Good night, Clayton. I'm staying in the other bedroom if you need me."

In a disappointing miracle, my Masters uniform is hanging in the closet, and everything else I need to be ready for school tomorrow is stacked on the desk. Figures Gran wouldn't skip a detail like prealgebra homework.

There's a phone on the nightstand, and I call Gran a couple of times on her cell, but she doesn't answer. I know she's not home, but I try there, too. I take the number Ms. Wynn gave me out of my pocket and put it on the dresser. It'll have to wait until tomorrow.

CHAPTER TWENTY-FIVE

The next morning I wake up earlier than usual. I shower and get dressed and report to Frankie with plenty of time to enjoy the waffles Gran promised. I stick my finger in the slot beside the closed elevator door, and while we wait for it to open, Frankie fixes my tie and gently pats my bald head.

"Have a nice day at school, Clayton," she says with a big smile as she nudges me into the elevator.

For some reason, when those words come out of Frankie's mouth, the simple sentence, "Have a nice day at school, Clayton," repeats in my brain again and again. I raise my hand back to her, wanting to say thanks—but I can't.

I quickly look down as the elevator door closes, and hide the two tears I tried really, really hard to stop from dropping out of my eyes.

I miss my mom. I miss my dad. I miss Gramps. Today of all days.

I growl my throat clear, trying to put my mind someplace else. It doesn't work until the elevator door opens and I walk out of the tiny closet into the diner's office—and see Carlos in Gran's chair, reading a newspaper. He smiles his most mischievous smile when he sees me, and the paper falls to his lap. "Clayton, my boy," he says. "You have been a busy young man."

In a single move he leaps to his feet and sticks out his hand for a shake. All the cells in my body come to a grinding halt. He *knows* about the elevator?

Even though I stand there like a dope, Carlos keeps his hand out and stares at me with the sort of expression you'd see on a cat who's overly pleased with himself. Like there's a dead mouse behind him somewhere.

I mean, it looks like Carlos. Same shaved head. Same white jacket and black pants. Same roguish sparkle in his eye. But something is different.

I stick out my hand and shake. "You would not believe how hungry I am," I say. "I think I could eat *three* waffles."

Carlos lets go of my hand, rubs my shaved head and gives me an approving nod. Then he heads out of the office with a wave for me to follow. "No, no, my boy. Not waffles. I have something very special for you this morning. Not every boy turns thirteen on Friday the thirteenth. Come to the kitchen, I've set a place for you there."

Whoa. My birthday is on Friday the thirteenth. Suddenly I'm glad I won't be going to the mall today.

"Carlos, *who* are you?" I say, jogging to stay with him.

He looks back and grunts with a quick raise of his eyebrows. "Carlos Enrico Luis Gonzales Smith," he says. "Why do you ask?"

"Smith? Are you kidding? And I wasn't asking about your name. I meant, who *are* you?"

He keeps moving and doesn't answer, so I trail after him through the bustling kitchen. We pass the grill cooks standing over sizzling bacon and eggs and pancakes, the busboys running in and out, gray tubs in their hands, then the food prep counter, where one guy's peeling potatoes and another is chopping carrots, and finally, the lady pouring a ten-pound bag of flour into the mixer—Carlos leads me all the way back to the farthest, narrowest part of the kitchen, to a small private counter where, a long time ago, I used to do homework. With a grand sweep of his hand, he gestures to the ornate place he's set for me, complete with crystal and linen and three pink roses in a vase. He whips a long, skinny grill lighter from inside his jacket and lights a tapered candle that's set right beside the flowers. Then he cocks his head and bats his eyes.

I shake my head and groan. "Very funny."

"Thank you," he says, looking at his watch. "Take a seat, your breakfast should be ready in a minute."

I put my backpack on the floor and sit. To the side of my empty, waiting plate is a dish with a huge stack of bacon and a small pitcher of syrup. And my cell phone. Huh. Captain Thompson's been here. I pick it up and put it in my pocket. Then, reluctantly, put the SpiPhone in its place.

I look up and Carlos is pulling a skillet out of the oven. The perimeter of the pan is eclipsed by a puffed and golden crust, and then whatever it is sinks low in the center, like a bowl. The aromas of the poofed thing, the bacon and the warm syrup make the juices in my stomach run expectantly.

Carlos slides the enormous concoction onto my plate, inhaling deeply. "This is called a Dutch baby. It's a giant puffed pancake."

I start to pick up my fork, but Carlos lifts his hand. "No, no. It's not finished." He takes the pitcher and drizzles maple syrup over the pancake. Next he scoops an enormous spoonful of berries into the sunken middle. Finally, he tops it with a dollop of whipped cream.

He steps back, opens his arms and bows. "Now, young man, you may eat."

He doesn't have to tell me twice. It's light and buttery, and when I take a bite of salty bacon, that makes it even better. Carlos just stands there with a huge grin on his face and watches me.

I stop chewing, but only for a second. I need an answer from him, and I mumble through my deliciously filled mouth. "Carlos, c'mon. You weren't surprised to see me appear out of the closet. What's going on? Who are you?"

Carlos's smile disappears. "I'm afraid that's classified infor-mation." Then he jerks his chin to the side and raises his eye-brows. "I can show you how to make one of these, though," he says, gesturing to my half-devoured Dutch baby.

I bend forward over my food and whisper. "Seriously, Car-los. You're part of . . . all of this, aren't you?"

He clucks his tongue. "What's your clearance, Clayton? Not-so-secret?"

I shrug. "Probably. They don't tell me much."

Carlos chuckles. "It's to protect you."

Now it's my turn to laugh. "So why do I keep ending up next to bad guys with guns?"

He stares at me for a second before he answers. "Good point. Finish your breakfast, I'm supposed to drive you to school."

I enjoy every single last bit of my breakfast while I watch Carlos bop around the kitchen and check in with his cooks and the rest of the staff.

I push my plate back and notice my SpiPhone is gone—Carlos sure has fast hands. All this time, he's been what? A head cook? An agent? I remember the time I asked Gramps why the kitchen was so crowded. He threw me one of his typical one-liners. *There are always potatoes to peel, Clayton.* Yeah, right.

I wonder what the "head cook" can tell me about booth number thirteen? "Hey, Carlos!"

He looks over from across the kitchen and holds up his finger.

Fine. I'll investigate myself. I get up, wipe my mouth and grab my backpack and lacrosse gear, but before I can even make it past the service counter, Carlos is walking with me, his arm squeezing my shoulders. "I told you I'd give you a ride. Where are you going?"

"Nowhere. I want to look at one of the booths, that's all."

He shakes his head. "Yeah, I'll bet you do," he says as we come around the corner and stop just feet away from booth thir-teen. Carlos may or may not be an undercover agent for the Spe-cial Service, but I'd recognize that gleam in his eyes anytime.

"What the heck? It *is* your birthday. Go sit down."

Huh? "Really? What are you going to do?"

Carlos's face is set to the serious channel. He shrugs. "Like I said, I'm supposed to take you to school. Just be sure to sit on the left side, not the right."

"Why?"

He shrugs again, smiling.

I take a step toward him. "But won't anybody notice?"

Carlos shakes his head as he walks away. "Not with me at the controls. Now move it, or you're going to be late no matter where you end up."

I very carefully sit down on the left side of the booth. There are so many people eating and moving around the diner, I don't know how he can be sure not one of them will notice.

A whole tray of dishes falls, clattering all over the floor somewhere in the front of the diner, and every single head in the room turns toward the commotion—away from booth thirteen. Almost simultaneously, the floor underneath me opens up and my bench seat releases and drops me onto a wide metal chute. I slide at least two floors down before I land smack in the middle of a huge square cushion, which is locked tight against the corner of a massive, well-lit parking garage.

I get up and throw my backpack and gear over my shoulder. *That* was cool. Now what?

Minutes pass. I'm about to text somebody—anybody—when I hear screeching tires making their way around the far end of the garage and see a black-as-night BMW hauling butt my way. Dang, that thing can move. I take a step back just as the car comes to a sixty-to-zero-in-less-than-three-seconds stop in the exact location where my toes had been.

The blacked-out window slides down and Carlos looks up at me with raised eyebrows. "What are you waiting for, Clayton? Get in."

I sit in the front seat, completely cramped because of all my stuff, and put on my seat belt. I mean, I always wear my seat belt, but right now I'm thinking it might actually be useful. And school is only ten minutes away.

Make that five with Carlos driving. My heart is pounding like a sledgehammer against my chest, and I can hardly breathe as he takes the final block at a NASCAR pace and peels into a horseshoe turn for an abrupt finish directly in front of Masters Academy.

Holy mother of burning rubber. I stare at him, my knuckles white and still gripping the door and the console. I've almost lost my lunch a dozen times this week, but this has to be the worst. "Carlos, have you considered driving school?"

He smirks and checks his watch. "Of course. I went to the best racing school in Germany. Top in my class. Why?"

Forget it. "No reason—just curious." I reach for my backpack and open the car door. "Thanks for the ride—and breakfast."

With a wink, he puts the car in gear. "Anytime, *amigo*. Now go have a happy birthday," he says. I shut the door, and before I can blink he's ripping around the corner at the far end of the street.

Racing school. It figures.

CHAPTER TWENTY-SIX

I walk though the school doors in time to hear my name blasting through the PA system. Awesome. For all the kids who don't care it's my birthday, now they know.

Toby's waiting in our spot, a mocha in each hand. I'm expecting some sort of smart remark about watching out for the inevitable birthday prank, but he doesn't even look at me as he hands me my drink. Weird. I'm getting nothing.

I guess things aren't quite back to normal. The whole Laci thing must really be bothering—I freeze. I can't believe it.

How the heck did I miss practice again yesterday?

Nobody remembered. Gran was too busy with the senator. The captain was distracted trying to track down the mall nappers and take me from place to place. And I, well, I *should* have remembered, no matter what was going on.

Crud. Triple crud.

Quadruple crud.

I cock my head and give Toby's face a hard look. His eyes are dull and droopy, like he got zero sleep last night. I don't want to ask, but I've got to start somewhere. "What's the matter?"

His tone is super-aggravated. "What is it with you? You

think you can show up for games, play the hero and that's it? Jeez, Clayton, you don't return texts anymore. Or calls. Every single time I try to get you this week, you're not around. What's the deal?"

He's got to get one thing straight. "I'm sorry. Really. But I didn't play the hero—you scored the game-winner. Remember?"

Toby shakes his head in disgust. "Whatever."

This really sucks. I mean, secrets are part of the deal. Gramps had to keep secrets. Gran, for sure, had to keep secrets. And my parents, too. So even though Toby's my best friend, I know I have to keep what I'm doing under wraps. Only, it's hard when—

A hand grabs my arm from behind. "Clayton, I need to ask you something."

I turn to see the person I was just thinking about. The person who knows what I'm doing with the Special Service. And she's staring at me with big green eyes, hesitating for a moment before she glances at Toby and then back at me. "In private?"

Toby's eyes are now wide awake and darting between me and Laci as if he's trying to figure out what's going on. He's not the only one. I'd give anything to be sitting in booth thirteen with Carlos at the controls so I could disappear into the floor. "Can it wait till lunch? I've got to get to homeroom."

She looks up at the giant clock on the wall. "Final bell doesn't ring for eight minutes, and this is important."

Toby starts to edge away from us, and I grab a piece of his blazer. "Wait, man," I say. I have to explain *something* to him.

He jerks out of my grasp and shakes his head. The confusion is gone, but something else has taken its place. "Nah," he says. "I get it. Happy birthday, Clayton. I'll see you in Davis's room."

I've got to fix whatever's going on, make Toby understand somehow, but he's walking down the hall without me.

Before I can go after him, Laci grabs the backs of my arms and pushes me across the atrium, through the double doors and into the gym. Sheesh. For a tiny girl, she's linebacker strong.

She takes her phone out of her backpack and holds it up to me. It's at this moment I realize she's serious. I mean, she's always serious about everything, but right now she's not-smiling serious.

"What's going on?" I say, looking from her to the phone in my face.

"I don't know. That's why I need you. I don't know if this is a joke or not."

I put my hand on her shoulder. "Laci, back up. You're going to have to explain this to me, from the beginning."

She nods. "Okay, well, I got a text this morning, from a strange number. I think it's from my friend, because we have this joke about how hot sauce sets her floor routine on fire— she always scores really high after she eats some. But none of this makes sense. I've been trying to text her. I've called her house a zillion times. Our coach called her dad's office every day this week and a lady finally told her she's on vacation with her mom."

I've never heard Laci sound so frantic. She's not talking sense, and I'm confused. "What does any of this have to do with me?"

Laci rolls her eyes and sighs. "Who else am I going to ask? Amber might be in trouble. You're the first person I thought of, you know, because of your 'job.' "

Huh. I guess that's kind of cool. Laci, the queen of Masters Academy, thinks I'm important; thinks I can help. I take the phone and look at the text, not sure what she's expecting, but what the heck?

I stop breathing. It's not the words that get my attention. It's the number. The one with the 202 area code. The number Ms. Wynn gave me. The number that sat on my dresser all night. And the number I put back in my pocket this morning. The very same number I'm supposed to give to Gran.

Holy mother of massive mistakes. That number Ms. Wynn gave me is important—major-important. My eyes lift reluctantly to meet Laci's, and Vesuvius-sized regret runs like red-hot lava into my belly. "What did you say your friend's name was?"

"Amber."

I close my eyes, as if that will stop everything.

"How do you know her?"

"She's on my gymnastics team—and she's my best friend. Why, Clayton? You know something? What's wrong?"

I know the answer to my next question. I don't even have to ask. "She's Senator Meldon's daughter, isn't she?"

Laci nods. "How do you know that? She doesn't tell anybody."

I let out a long sigh. "Laci, she and her mom have been missing all week. That's what I've been doing. Trying to help find her. She's been kidnapped, and it's all part of the napper crimes."

My eyes drop back to Amber's message.

Get police. 911. We're in a basement. Jerk wants us dead. Hot sauce.

Laci's eyes are shining, ready to spill over. "She's been kidnapped?"

Oh, crud. Please don't cry. "Yeah. But this is good, because now we know she's alive."

Laci shakes her head. "No, it's not good. I thought they were stuck in the basement at her house or something."

I'm confused all over again. "Why would they be stuck in their own house?"

"Because the senator is her stepfather and she calls him 'the jerk.'"

I look at the number and read the text again. This is not good. I remember Gran talking to the captain about wanting to question the senator. And they couldn't because—why? And what did Ms. Wynn say? She could be fired—or worse. More crud.

Get police. 911. That's simple. It's an emergency and she needs help.

We're in a basement. An address would have been better, but okay.

Jerk wants us dead. Seriously bad news if the jerk is the senator.

Hot sauce. Hot sauce? Okay, Laci says it's a joke, but if you're in danger, why would you be joking around? All I can think of is when Ms. Wynn told me Amber loves hot sauce and orders by the bucket when she gets fried chicken.

I don't have time to figure this out. A rush of adrenaline shoots through my body—I've got to get moving. I give Laci her phone and start for the door. "Did you text her back?"

She follows me. I can tell she's trying to get control, but her thoughts are all over the place. "No, it's not her number. I didn't know what to do."

"Good. Don't. And don't do anything. It might get her hurt. Somehow she got his phone. I sure hope she erased that text after she sent it."

As I push through the doors, I hand Laci my still-full mocha. Kids race past in spurts of ones and twos, bypassing my backpack and lacrosse gear still on the floor in the middle of the atrium. The bell's going to ring in seconds. I hurry over and pick up my backpack, then face Laci, who's only a step behind. She's trembling now, and I can see she needs something to do. "Can you take my lacrosse stuff to Mr. Davis's room and give it to Toby? And anybody who asks, tell them I'm doing something, uh, for student government, okay?"

Her mouth drops open as she takes my bag. "You're leaving school? What are you going to do?"

"I'm going to try to get them help. But I have to go *now,* Laci."

"Clayton—can I come?" She lets my lacrosse gear fall to the floor and the tears begin to stream down her cheeks. "I have to help. She's my best friend."

I reach down for my bag and firmly stick the straps back in her hands. Gran will kill me if I involve Laci in this. "No," I say. Then I grab my cell out of my pocket. "You can help. What's your number?"

She tells me and I plug it in my phone and call her. "Now you can get me, Laci—anytime—and keep checking yours. I'll let you know what's going on if I can." I look around the atrium, the uptight school I've always thought was too restrictive. Now I'm glad it is. "Here you're safe, and that's important, because I may need you."

I hike up my backpack and hustle backward out the main door. As I make my way down the massive stone steps, Laci calls to me. "Be careful," she says.

When I reach the sidewalk, I turn back to her, my cell phone in the air. "Don't worry. It'll be okay."

Laci's shoulders relax, like she believes me. She thinks I'm going to bring back her friend. I watch her disappear behind the Masters doors and then I dial Gran. Again.

No answer.

I look up and down the street and realize there's a big black hole in my rescue plan. I don't know where Amber and her mom are. All I have is a crumpled phone number with a 202 area code.

Gran's not home and she's not answering her phone, but she's in the middle of all this—so I have to get to her somehow. I don't know how to get in touch with the captain, not without my SpiPhone, at least. My best bet is headquarters. If Gran's not there, somebody will help me find her.

The only way I know to get to the Special Service is through the diner. I pivot and head due north to Big Stone's. Home of the famous BS pickles.

CHAPTER TWENTY-SEVEN

I run. Wearing my navy blazer. My tie. My school shoes. Carrying my backpack. It's as comfortable as sprinting in bubble wrap, but after the first thirty seconds it doesn't matter. I don't know Amber or her mom, but it's all coming together in my head and nobody has to tell me they're in deep.

They weren't kidnapped by mistake. The deal is, they're alive by mistake.

I cross Glebe Road, praying I don't get flattened by some idiot checking e-mail on their way to work. When I make it to the other side, I scroll to Gran's number on my cell and press Call. Twenty rings, no answer and no message picks up. I don't get it. She always answers my calls. Always. And why can't I leave a message?

I keep going, only slowing my pace to jog across the stop-and-go jam of Friday-morning traffic. When Big Stone's is finally in sight, I realize something. I have no clue how to get to the Special Service offices by myself. I've never worked the elevator in the closet without Gran, and even if I manage to drop through booth thirteen, how do I get from the pillow pad landing to the offices? I could be stuck in the garage until—it's too late.

I need Carlos.

I take the concrete steps two at a time and burst into the diner breathing hard. The hostess comes toward me with menus in her hand and then stops. "Clayton? What are you doing here?"

I brush past her and hurry down the aisle, calling behind me, "I forgot something."

The kitchen is still busy with the breakfast rush, and I scan the white jackets for Carlos. I walk past all the cooks, willing him to appear. I'm about to give up and resort to other options, like searching behind the Dumpsters, when Carlos materializes out of the walk-in fridge.

When he sees me, he freezes and his lips tighten against his teeth in a wary smile. An instant later, he's got his arm around me and he's guiding me into the walk-in. "What happened?"

"Do you know what I'm working on with Gran and Captain Thompson?"

Carlos shakes his head. "All I know is you brought two of the mall nappers in."

At this point I don't care what I'm supposed to keep secret. I need help. "They have Senator Meldon's wife and daughter."

"The mall nappers?"

"Yeah," I say.

"Did you see the news this morning?"

"No, why?"

"The senator was on all the morning shows, talking about the kidnapping. He said the kidnappers were threatening to kill his family."

"This is the thing. He's in on it. The senator *knows* the kidnappers."

Carlos looks at me so hard his eyebrows intersect over his nose. "How do you know that?"

I pull the piece of paper with the phone number Ms. Wynn gave me out of my pocket. "Because the senator's assistant gave me this number. I was supposed to give it to Gran yesterday. I didn't understand at the time, but now I do. This is the personal number of the same guy who called about the ransom for the senator's family. The senator has talked to him before, and so has his assistant. That's why she recognized the voice." I hold the piece of paper in the air and add, "*This* is the guy who has the senator's family."

"You didn't give it to your grandmother?"

I shake my head. "She's been busy working on the kidnapping. I should have gotten it to her somehow. I blew it. I didn't think—"

Carlos pulls me out of the fridge and boogies me back through the kitchen. As we turn the corner and head for the office, he leans close to me. "You haven't blown it, Clayton, they're still alive," he says. He must have had something on his eggs this morning, because—

Holy mother of hot sauce. Of course. They've been eating food from Big Stone's. It definitely wasn't a joke. Amber was trying to tell Laci something. I break Carlos's hold and shift into reverse. "We've gotta look at all the orders," I say, frantic, unsure of which way to go. "Carryout and delivery, for the whole week. Do you know where they are?"

Carlos doesn't waste time asking questions. "No," he says, already a blur ahead of me. "But I can find out."

He catapults himself into the dining room and shouts, "Conchita!"

Conchita, the floor manager, looks up like a raccoon caught in a garbage can, her dark eyes reacting to Carlos's urgent call, the rest of her frozen over the papers in front of her. "*¿Sí?*"

He answers her in a furious string of Spanish, and within thirty seconds she's following us back to the office with a huge accordion file in her arms.

She sits at Gran's desk and starts removing receipts from the file, then gestures to Carlos and commands him as if she's a four-star general. "My laptop, now. Log in under 'carryout' and pull up 'orders' starting with last Sunday." She turns to me. "What are we looking for, Clayton?"

What, is the diner Special Service Central? These agents

sure morph easy. I drop my backpack and sit. Then I swallow and shake my head a little to reactivate my brain. "Uh, fried chicken and extra hot sauce. Maybe a bucket, but at least a lot of packets. And maybe triple-berry pie?"

Conchita nods, her eyes never leaving the receipts flying through her fingers at card-shark speed. "Do you have that, Vlad?"

"Got it," Carlos says, his eyes locked on the computer screen.

"Vlad? As in Vladimir?" I say.

The edge of Conchita's lip turns. "Do yourself a favor and don't get hung up on names in this business, Clayton."

Before I can respond, Carlos erupts from his chair. "Got it," he says, and reaches for the sheets of paper jetting out of the printer. "Three days this week. Basically the same chicken orders, all with extra hot sauce. Last two times a bucket was requested. A couple of burgers, and other dinners. Pie, too. Delivered to the same address—cash only." He looks straight into my eyes and hands me the printouts. "The only orders this week requesting hot sauce with the chicken. The address and phone number are on top."

I stare down at the papers in my hand. Oh, crap! The phone number matches the one Ms. Wynn gave me.

What the heck do I do now? Think, Clayton. *Think!*

"I need to find Gran," I say to Carlos. "Like, yesterday."

Carlos is in the closet before I can stand up, maneuvering the same way Gran did only a few days ago. I follow him and enter the elevator before the wall is completely open. I stick my finger into the control panel and follow the directions that come up on the screen. I look up to see Carlos, still inside the closet.

"Aren't you coming?"

Carlos looks at his watch. "Find Frankie. I've got to deal with something here—but I'll follow you down in ten minutes and take you to your grandmother. Clayton, do not, and I repeat, *do not* leave this building without me."

As he disappears behind the sliding wall, all I can think is, Right now ten minutes seems like a really long time.

CHAPTER TWENTY-EIGHT

The elevator doors take forever to open, and I push through the second they crack apart. I scramble across the huge center room, moving as fast as my legs will carry me.

I make it all the way across the shining concrete floor and then stop. The wall to Gran's office is closed. I turn and scan the place. A blond woman stands up from a computer screen, and for a second I think it's Agent Moxie—but it's not. She walks right past me. Nope—nobody I recognize. My eyes fall to the seating area where Gran and I had our first real conversation about the Special Service. And where I ate last night.

Carlos is right; Frankie's the only one who will know where Gran is. I run up the hall and stick my head through the first doorway. Sure enough, she's there, sitting at a desk. She looks up from what she's doing and raises her eyebrows.

"Frankie, I need Gran. Do you know where she is?"

"Come in, Clayton," she says as she gets out of her chair and comes toward me. "What's the matter? Why aren't you in school?"

There's no time, so I have to tell her everything. Almost everything. "You know the senator's wife and daughter?"

She crosses her arms and tilts her head, waiting for me to continue.

"I think I know where they are. I need Gran. Please! Can you help me?"

"Clayton, your grandmother told me, *adamantly*, that your part in this is over. You did a great job, but now it's in her hands. She and Captain Thompson have been with the senator all night. They're negotiating with the kidnappers. And since they won't stay on the line longer than thirty seconds—and they immediately turn their phone off after each call—we can't trace the signal."

She takes me by the hand like a little kid and leads me back to the door. "It's going to take a while to track them down. We just want to keep you safe—your grandmother doesn't need to worry about you while she does her job. So don't you think you should be getting back to school?"

She's not listening. I shake away from her, wondering where Carlos is. *He* could convince her. "Seriously, Frankie, I can help! I think I know where the kidnappers are holding them. But it's complicated. I have to talk to Gran. I've tried calling her, but I can't get through. She always answers my calls. Is something wrong?"

"No, Clayton. Nothing is wrong. The chief is extremely busy and, as I said, gave me strict orders. You are to go to school and stay out of this entire operation from here on out. I know you want to help, but your grandmother is my boss."

I look down at the receipts Carlos gave me and then finger the paper in my pocket. I don't want to get Ms. Wynn in trouble—she told me, *only* Gran—but how else am I gonna get the number to Gran? How else am I gonna let Frankie know that all this time when Gran said they should question him, she was right—the tan senator with the snow-white smile *is* one of the bad guys.

I pull the phone number out of my pocket. "Fine," I say, slapping the paper into Frankie's hand along with one of the diner receipts. "Here's the number they should be looking at, and the address of the place I think they're holding the Meldons. Tell Gran to ask Ms. Wynn." I charge out of the office, then turn back to make one last attempt. "And by the way, the senator wanted them kidnapped."

"Clayton," Frankie says, shaking her head. "Where are you going?"

I give up. She's not going to help me, so I'm on my own. "Where do you want me to go?" I say, taking big strides down the hall.

"School would be nice. Do you need a ride?"

I shake my head and look down at the address on the receipt still in my hands. "No, Carlos will take me."

I check over my shoulder to see if Frankie is following; her door is already shut.

How many minutes have passed since Carlos said "ten minutes"?

I turn the corner and sprint across the main room to where the elevator is, about thirty yards away. I will the doors to open and Carlos to appear.

They don't.

He doesn't.

Thirty seconds later, still nothing. Could he be in the garage?

I look at the ceiling. The elevator is underneath Gran's diner office. There's the hall, the kitchen and then the actual restaurant. Booth thirteen would be about...I look to my left and across the room. Sure enough, there's a hallway. I glide like a reconnaissance drone and try every door down the line. This has to be the right spot.

It is. The last door I try opens to bleak walls of concrete and lines of parked cars.

I push into the parking garage, keeping an eye out for a speeding BMW. *Where* is Carlos? There're rows and rows of cars, and some of them have to be Special Service vehicles. I heard some of the agents talking about how they like driving the new agency cars.

It's got to be way past ten minutes. Amber and her mom can't wait much longer. A couple of cars up, I see Carlos's BMW, and it occurs to me—I drove once. In a field. On Gramps's lap. But still, I drove. How much different is an actual road?

I stare at the BMW, and a plan starts to form in my brain. I mean, I can't drive a stick or whip a 180 like Carlos, but—I start moving down the row of cars, ticking them off: Porsche, Ferrari, Lamborghini. Holy mother of speeding tickets. I thought this was an undercover agency. Where are the cars that blend in?

I start running down the line and move across to the next row, praying I find something normal, like a Ford or Chevy.

I stop at a gray Subaru wagon; it's as close as I'm gonna get.

I peer inside the driver's-side window, instantly relieved; it looks like an automatic. I check the door, and just like in every spy movie I've ever seen, it's unlocked and the keys are dangling from the ignition.

This is what Gramps used to call "meant to be." I get in, shut the door and hold my breath as I stretch my toes to reach the pedals. Not quite.

I drop my left hand to the door controls and move the seat up and forward. It works.

I have no idea where the house is, but I do know how to use navigation. I turn the key one click. The screen lights up and the electronics start to chime. I press the button that says Destination, then key in the street and the house number, something I do all the time for Gran. When the route comes up on the map I feel better, but only until I look at the steering wheel, the gearshift, and the instrument panel and realize I don't know what the heck to do next.

I think I turn the key all the way first, but—I've never done *that*. I hang my head and close my eyes. What do I do? When I open my eyes, I'm looking at the dark-blue stripes of my tie. My tie. If I can learn to tie a tie on the Internet—my fingers can't press the browser app on my phone fast enough.

The search box appears and I type in: *Learn to drive a car.*

I pick a video and stand the phone in the cup holder as the lesson begins.

- **Brake is the pedal on the left. Accelerator pedal is on the right.**
- **Press the brake pedal.**
- **Turn the key in the ignition.**
- **With foot still on brake, move gearshift from "PARK" position to "DRIVE" or "REVERSE."**
- **Press accelerator pedal with steady, firm effort until you reach desired speed.**

Okay, I can do that.

I press the brake and turn the key hard, and the engine hums. Good.

I move the gearshift into drive and slowly take my foot from the brake pedal and place it on the accelerator, pressing very lightly.

Nothing. The car sits there.

I press the accelerator a little harder and the engine gives a whoosh and moves forward about an inch. This is getting nowhere.

My eyes scan the parking garage for Carlos.

Dang it. I just have to go for it.

I grip hard on the steering wheel and rest my chin between my hands, like an old lady driver. Barely breathing, I tense my entire leg and press the pedal hard; with a sudden pop, the Subaru lurches forward ten feet as my foot scrambles to the brake. I jam on the brake pedal and miraculously miss the bumper of the car parked directly across the lot.

And now I gotta back up, because if I keep going forward, I will hit that car. I look closer. Nope. Don't want to even breathe near a Lamborghini.

My foot is on the brake, so I'm pretty sure it's safe to shift into reverse.

Three inches at a time, I finally make it down to the garage exit, the navigation lady repeating her directions with every turn of the car. I'd turn her annoying voice off, but I have a feeling I'm going to need her.

It's here: the real road. I can feel the vein in my neck, pulsing hard through my skin. What am I gonna do when I get to the house? I don't have my SpiPhone. I don't have any sedative sticks, and Gran made sure to take the stun pen away from me. I don't have bugs crawling on me from head to toe, and no GPS plastered in my underwear, either.

For a Special Service agent, I'm practically naked. Goose bumps prickle my arm and put me on high alert.

I should think twice about this. Or three times. I should turn around and wait for Carlos. Or raid Gran's supply closet. Or scream.

But Amber and her mom might be out of time. I know I have to go. I'll spy on the house, and if they're there, I'll call the police. The Subaru is the color of fog; I should be able to drive without anybody blinking. I mean, it's not like arriving in the fluorescent-red Porsche.

I look both ways—nobody. I slip my foot to the gas pedal, and with a deep breath and a steady-as-I-can-manage push, I'm off.

Next stop: Napper Avenue.

CHAPTER TWENTY-NINE

For the record, driving on actual streets is totally different than driving on a country field or on Xbox. There's no possible way anybody can read so many signs—and cars, beside me, behind me, coming toward me, all going the honkin' speed of sound.

Seriously. What's that guy thinking, walking right in front of me?

Red Light! Stop!!!

I slam the brake so hard my entire body jerks—first against my seat belt and then back again so my head rams the headrest with the force of a bowling ball.

Half a dozen close calls and a missed stop sign later, I make it. According to the navigation lady, the house is directly ahead on the left. I steer toward a car parked on the side of the road, aiming to pull directly behind it. The passenger side of the Subaru starts to tilt like the see end of a saw. My aim is obviously off. Not only have I skipped the curb, I think I've nailed the sidewalk pretty good, too.

I take out my phone and dial Gran again. Still no answer, and right now I'm kicking myself. Carlos has the address, but will he figure out that I actually got here? O.M.G. I should have his number. I should be able to get in touch with Gran. And it shouldn't have mattered what Ms. Wynn said, or that Frankie didn't believe me.

I want to bang my head on the steering wheel, 'cause I don't know what to do. What if—the second the question forms, I can practically hear Gran tell me, like she did two days ago, it doesn't matter about what *might* happen. I have to deal with "what *is*." And in this moment, "what is" is very clear: lives are on the line.

So how am I gonna fix what *is*?

One thing's for sure, I need help. But who? And how?

A memory of Laci flashes in front of me. She's in the observation room with her mom and Captain Thompson, and she's taking Captain Thompson's card. I poke my phone and I can't believe it. There she is. A text from a few minutes ago.

Where r u?

It's the weirdest thing. Of all the people in the entire world, she's the only one who can help me.

CALL CPT THOMPSON NOW. GIVE HIM THAT NUMBER.

I hesitate for a second. If I'm wrong and this isn't where the senator's daughter is, I'm up the Special Service creek, but if I'm right, I need backup. Now. There's only one way I'm gonna get it, 'cause I can't count on Frankie.

I type in the address and send it to Laci. Then I add:

TELL HIM I NEED HELP.

Now there's a chance, but there's something else. How can I go in without a weapon? I'm in a Special Service car. Huh. Could there be—

I open the glove compartment, afraid and hopeful at the same time. And there it is. Not a stun pen or a sedative stick. A gun. A real gun.

I shouldn't. I know that. Only, there isn't a choice, and I know that, too. I shut the door on every single instinct telling me not to. Right or wrong, there's no time for doubts. I grab the gun.

I'm amazed at how something so small can feel so heavy; this strange piece of metal can kill in an instant. I don't know much about guns, but Gramps taught me one thing, in case I ever came across one: there's usually a way to keep it from accidentally firing. A shiver goes through me as I rotate the safety from *F* to *S*. I stick it in my jacket pocket and open the car door.

I walk across the street and step up to the sidewalk, counting the houses, looking for the number: 23701.

All these houses, with their trees and parked cars, one after the other, are so ordinary. But bricks and shingles can hide secrets. And there it is—23701—the house with the biggest secret of all.

"Please, God," I say in a whisper as I creep along the neighbor's hedge on the left side of the house.

The yard is overgrown, but I spot a small window well toward the back—a way to look in the basement. My heart beats triple-time as I move toward it, and I rub the gun in my pocket. It doesn't make me feel any better.

It's quiet, except for the crackle of my shoes on the vines. I lean against the brick, a few yards from the window. So far, it's okay. No voices, no doors opening. Nothing. In a last surge, I dive over the final mound of foliage and land hard on my stomach, inches shy of the tiny concrete pit. I drag myself forward with my elbows and squint to see through the grimy glass.

I don't know what Amber or her mom looks like, but I'm staring at two females with their hands tied, pacing back and forth in a crumbly, dilapidated old basement. They've got tired eyes and flattened hair, and I'd bet every toy in Gran's arsenal it's them. Who else can it be?

I take out my phone and start dialing. I get as far as 9-1 when the familiar chill of metal against my neck paralyzes every bit of me.

A crusty, irritated voice rumbles next to my ear. "So I wanna know what a bald kid in a fancy getup is doing gropin' around my yard."

He snatches the phone out of my hands and pulls me up by the scruff of my blazer. A string of curses whistles through his lips as he hauls me around back and up some rickety wooden stairs. We enter the house through a screen door propped partway open with a cinder block. Stairs to the basement are on the left, but we take two steps up to the first floor and the kitchen. The counters are lined with cruddy glasses and plates and there's a thick layer of foamy scum floating on top of the water in the sink. A heap of overflowing garbage bags is piled in the corner behind a white plastic table that's covered with a mess of maps, a ton of broken peanut shells and at least a dozen cell phones, each a different size and color. The captain was right. They must be using a different phone every time they call.

My shoes stick to the floor as the guy pushes me along; I stumble, sending a Big Stone's carryout box across the room. He wings me around to face him, but all I can register is the big, black gun he has pointed at me.

"Hey! Roger! Look what I found."

Roger enters the kitchen and stares at me. His entire neck is a matrix of brightly colored designs that stretch all the way up to his ears. He turns sharply to the guy who nabbed me. "Lee, are ya nuts? Why would ya—"

Lee shakes his head and his stringy blond hair falls across his eyes. "Now wait a minute," he says, brushing his hair back with the gun. Then he wags the weapon at me. "He was lookin' in the basement—what was I supposed to do?"

"Tell him to scat, whaddya think? This is gettin' bad enough. Wheeler and Dempsey are in jail, we got those two downstairs, and Meldon's on the news tryin' to put the whole dang thing on us. Now you bring another kid into it?" Roger tailspins out of the room and then freezes.

He turns his head and stares at me, and then he steps closer and narrows his eyes as they travel from my head to my shoes. "What're ya doing nosin' around here?"

I scramble for something. Anything. "I was, uh, late to

school and trying to take a shortcut through your back yard." Lame.

Roger searches the room with his eyes, and his tattoos twist and bend like a kaleidoscope. The expression on his face is a little twisted, too, his forehead furrowing like he's thinking real hard—and it's painful. "And what's with the jacket 'n' tie? Ya goin' to a weddin'?"

I shrug. "It's my uniform." I don't want to say anything else.

"You with the senator? The police?" Roger gets in my face and Lee, following Roger's lead, takes another step toward me and puts the gun to my head. "Tell the truth, kid. Does anybody know where we are?"

I shake my head and, too late, realize I shouldn't have. Roger's eyes widen.

Lee tosses my phone to Roger. "He was making a call when I got him."

Roger starts poking at the unfamiliar screen but gives up after a minute. It's easy to tell, he just doesn't want to deal with me.

He grabs my arm and yanks me hard through some sort of living room. There's a television on an upside-down box, a lamp with a T-shirt thrown over the shade, and a floor covered with blankets and pillows and duffel bags, some of them overflowing with clothes and money—lots and lots of money. We stumble through the mess and he muscles me to the right, down a narrow hallway. He wrenches my arm and pushes me against the wall, simultaneously jerking my hands together. "Cut me some of that rope, Lee!" he shouts. My whole body starts to tremble; I can't help it. What's he gonna do, strangle me?

Lee shows up with a piece of rope, his stringy hair swinging across his face as he moves. He doesn't even bother to push it back as he hands the rope to Roger and watches while Roger ties my hands in back of me. Real tight.

The place where Roger had been gripping me aches and my wrists burn, but I know he could have used that rope for something else—

"Where we gonna put him, the john?" says Lee.

"What do *you* think, Einstein? It's the only bathroom in the house," says Roger. He turns me around and I try to look him in the eyes, but I keep getting sucked in by the tattoos all linked together on his neck. Is it one picture, or a bunch of little ones? I see letters, and I'm about to focus on them when he grabs my arm again and slings me toward Lee. "Put him downstairs. And don't talk to those girls this time."

Lee takes me, sputtering back to Roger the whole way. "I wasn't gonna let 'em go. They just said their wrists hurt, so I loosened the rope."

"You listen to me and stay away, or I'm gonna throw you down there with 'em. Ya hear?"

"I hear you," says Lee. He pushes me around the corner and stops in the middle of the kitchen. "We got enough cash. Why don't we get out and leave them?"

Roger follows us into the kitchen and grabs a couple of peanuts. "You really are an idiot. The real cash is coming! And if we kill 'em, Meldon says we get triple. But we can't do it here—'cause they're never gonna put me away for murder again. That means no evidence." He pauses and eats the peanuts while he stares at us, the shells dropping to the floor. "You got zero brain cells, but you're right. We gotta get outta here."

Lee turns me toward the back doorway and shoves me forward again. Three things I know. These guys love peanuts, they're slobs, and they're definitely working with Senator Meldon.

Lee forces me down the stairs and unlocks the door at the bottom. He opens it and I stumble into a shadowy room—the one I saw from the window?

I start to look around when something comes at me fast and my body slams into the cinder-block wall.

I shut down like a dead cell phone.

CHAPTER THIRTY

My body aches. My head is pounding. The floor is rough and cold. And there are wobbly voices whispering over me.

I squint my closed eyes even more closed, trying to understand what they're saying.

"I think he's waking up."

There's a hand on my shoulder. "Are you okay?"

I can't speak yet, so I breathe a noise out of my mouth, like a hum. Then a grunt. Finally, I open my eyes. It wasn't a hand touching me. It was a forehead.

Amber and her mom both straighten up and stare. Mrs. Meldon's eyes are smeared with black and her hair is pushed back in a flattened mess of curls. She's wearing a pantsuit that probably started out cream-colored but now has the "I've been living in my car" look. Amber's blond hair hangs long and straight, and the jeans and dark-blue shirt she's wearing aren't nearly as crumpled as her mom's clothes. But the dark circles under her eyes tell me she's exhausted, too.

It's obvious they've been stuck in this basement for a week. They stink—big-time.

Their hands are tied behind their backs, and Amber struggles as she gets to her feet. "Did they take you from a mall?"

I shake my head. "No. I was looking for you. You're Senator Meldon's daughter."

Amber snorts. "*Step*daughter."

Oh. But wait. "Isn't your last name Meldon?"

"My real dad died when I was a baby. Mom thought she was doing me a favor by making my last name the same as hers."

I turn to Mrs. Meldon, who couldn't look more sorry for officially making her daughter a "Meldon." "It was an election year, and he thought it would be good to present ourselves as a family unit."

She stares at me with a doubtful expression. "You were searching for us? Who are you?"

"My name's Clayton. And it's a long story. But I'm here to help, and I hope the Special Service is on its way."

Mrs. Meldon shakes her head. "They won't come. My husband will stop them somehow. Those nitwits upstairs talked right in front of us. He wants us dead and out of his life so he can have control of my business assets and all my money. He planned the entire thing—all the mall muggings, the kidnappings—so our murders could be covered up."

Of course. *She's* the rich one. If she dies *and* her daughter dies, he gets it all. Not only is Senator Meldon involved, he's the one who arranged everything. *Everything.*

The senator must have hired these bozos to take moms with kids at the malls, so that when they kidnapped Mrs. Meldon and Amber, nobody would think to blame him. Or ask him any questions at all. The police, the Special Service—even the president— all feel sorry for the "jerk." The mall crimes have made his wife's kidnapping look like a crime gone wrong—or right.

Gran was the only one who ever said the senator should be investigated. And now I see how right she was.

"He's gonna get caught, Mrs. Meldon."

Amber's eyebrows swirl a question mark up the center of her forehead. "How did you figure out how to find us?"

"The message you sent Laci Peters. It was what you said

about hot sauce. Great clue, by the way." I look around the crumbling old basement. "What I want to know is, how the heck did you send that text?"

Amber and her mom look at each other. "They let us use the bathroom twice a day, and eat once. Those are the only times they untie us," says Amber, keeping her voice low. "This morning I went into the bathroom and there was a cell phone on the sink. So I texted Laci as quick as I could, and then I erased it so they wouldn't see."

I look up to the shaking ceiling. There's a lot of stomping going on up there. Whatever they've decided to do is happening in a hurry.

"How long have I been—uh, lying here?"

"Not long. Maybe a few minutes," says Amber, looking down at me.

Mrs. Meldon puts her face right up to mine. "Clayton. Does *anybody* besides you actually know where we are?"

I wish I could answer that question. Carlos knows, but he never showed up. Maybe *he* found Gran. "There's an agent who knows. And I gave Laci the address, and she's calling Captain Thompson at the Special Service. He'll show up."

I say it not because I believe it, but because I have to believe it. How the heck am I gonna go against two armed guys, all by myself? I feel a clunk as I push myself up and lean against the wall.

How could I forget? Talk about luck. They never patted me down.

I meet Mrs. Meldon's worried gaze. "I have a gun," I whisper.

She looks toward the noises coming from the ceiling. "You can have a trunkful of guns, but it's not going to do us any good while we're locked down here with our hands tied. If my husband has anything to do with it, the Special Service won't come—and it's only a matter of time before they kill us."

I wish she were wrong. "We have to—"

She throws her shoulders up in a hopeless shrug. "There are

two of them, Clayton. And they each have guns, and two work-ing hands. How do you expect to—"

She's the one who told me, and she still doesn't understand.

"You're right. Except being right doesn't matter. They're going to leave this house, and they're going to take us with them. Mostly because they're afraid of leaving evidence that can send them to prison. Plus, they won't get their money unless they *finish* the job." I stare hard at her for a few seconds before I clear my throat and point out the very obvious bad news. "Who's paying these guys?"

She sighs. "I told you. My husband is."

I raise my eyebrows. "And what is he paying them to do?"

She doesn't answer, just keeps looking at me.

"They aren't going to let us live, Mrs. Meldon. So, yeah, if we try to get away, there's a chance somebody gets hurt. But if we don't do anything, they control what happens one hundred percent."

Mrs. Meldon frowns as she nods back at me. "Okay. But do you have any ideas?"

I close my eyes and think. It won't do any good if we try to attack them in this basement. Or anywhere in this house. They're planning to take us somewhere. The only way they can do that is if they put us in a car. And with our hands tied, we won't be able to do much more than shout for help and hope one of the neighbors hears us. We need something better than that. Like a defensive move on the lacrosse field that turns into an offensive play. Laci is counting on me to help her friend.

I swing my head to Amber. "You're a gymnast, like Laci. Right?"

"Yeah," she says.

"So you can get probably get your hands in front of you?"

Amber tilts her head and frowns. "I guess. But it won't matter. We've already tried to untie each other—the knots are too tight."

I yank on my wrists. "Yeah, I know. Only, think about it. Either Roger or Lee is going to have to drive. A person can't drive and hold a gun at the same time. So if we plan it right, it will be three against one."

"I'm not following," says Mrs. Meldon.

I turn to her. "They're keeping our hands tied behind us so we don't have any leverage. But if one of us can somehow get our arms over the head of whoever's driving, the strength of the rope will actually help. We just choke him until he stops the car." I shrug at the confused look on her face. "Or something like that, anyway."

Amber's eyes suddenly light up. "Mom, Clayton's right! I can get these in front of me. Watch." She squats to the floor and curls up like a roly-poly bug, steps over her tied hands and holds them in front of her. Then, just as quickly, she puts her hands behind her back again.

"All right," says Mrs. Meldon, looking back and forth between us, her tone still doubtful. "But what about you, Clayton? I doubt you've been trained to use a gun with your hands tied."

I figure I better skip the fact that I've never been trained to use a gun—period. I turn away from her and scan the room, looking for something, I'm not sure what. There's a table with a couple of chairs pushed under it at the end of the room. Some leftover food and drinks on top of it. A pile of blankets near the table. Absolutely nothing I can use. My eyes follow the ground across the unfinished floor, to the cinder-block walls, to the windows, up high and set deep, with sharp ledges. And as I look at the windows, a scene from a show I used to watch as a kid comes to me, where the superspy saws his hands free from duct tape.

The echo of footsteps continues to sound from above, and I know it won't be much longer till they make their way down the stairs again. "Help me with this chair," I say, moving to the table. "I have an idea."

Amber and her mom are right behind me. "Where?" says Amber.

I nod to the window that looks like it has the sharpest ledge.

"Over there," I say, bumping the chair out from under the table with my foot and my hip.

Mrs. Meldon turns around, grips the top of the chair with her fingers and starts dragging as I push. Amber steps back but moves with us, bracing it with her body so it doesn't fall over as we move across the jagged concrete floor.

We finally get it to the wall and, crouching the way Amber did earlier, I hurdle over my bound hands so they're in front of me. Then I balance my forearms against the cinder block and carefully step up so I'm standing on the seat of the chair. "Hold the chair steady, okay?"

I lean the rope that binds my wrists together against the edge of the sill and begin a slow and steady grind in a seesaw motion.

I keep going until I can't hold my arms up anymore, and I examine the rope.

A few pretty strong threads are still connected, but with the right momentum I should be able to break free. I hope, anyway. It's not something I can worry about now, because the clock is ticking.

I jump to the floor and quickly put my hands behind me again.

The Meldons haven't said a word the entire time, and I motion them away from the chair. We don't dare get caught dragging it back to the table. Roger and Lee will show, in seconds or minutes. Who knows?

We need all the time we can get, because what if Gran didn't get the message? Or what if Laci didn't get in touch with Captain Thompson? Then maybe the Special Service won't come. And maybe me getting free, getting to my gun, is our only chance.

At the sound of heavy footsteps on the stairs, the three of us look at each other and back against the far wall.

It'll pretty much come down to one shot.

CHAPTER THIRTY-ONE

I don't breathe as the knob rattles and the door bursts open.

It's the guy named Lee, and he's waving his monster gun. "Okay, let's go. And I'm warnin' you. No yellin', no talkin', no nuttin' from none of ya. Don't make me use this thing. I don't care if ya live or ya die, but I don't wanna clean up a big mess."

We walk up the stairs to where Roger is waiting at the screen door. He moves out of the house into the backyard and sort of tucks his gun into his jacket so it's pointed at us but nosy neighbors can't see. His sour expression tells me he's not as indifferent as his friend Lee about our breathing status. Roger absolutely can't wait to cut off our O$_2$.

They push us into the garage next to the house, where there's a huge Cadillac with rusty plates. Lee opens the back passenger-side door and gestures for us to get into the backseat. Then Roger raps the top of the car with his gun. "You idiot! We can't have all of 'em together. We gotta separate 'em." He looks straight at me. "Boy, I'm takin' you. Get up front."

I don't know whether this is good or bad, but I'm not exactly in a man-up position, so I do what he says. As I duck into the front seat, I get a glimpse of a black baseball cap as it steals past the garage window. Captain Thompson?

Could the good guys be here?

I twist to look back at Amber and Mrs. Meldon, hoping to signal: *Something's up!* They're sitting together and Lee's beside them, right behind me. He sneers and says, "Turn yer butt around." I face front.

Roger starts the car, and my heart is beating so fast it could power the lights on the national Christmas tree. Whatever is going to happen is going to happen soon.

Roger lights a cigarette and lowers the window partway. He shifts the car into reverse and starts to back out of the garage. I need to distract him from anything that might be happening outside the car. "Uh, don't you think we should be wearing seat belts?" I say.

"Shut up" is the only response I get. That and a mumbled round of curses.

I don't know how Amber is going to get her hands in front of her. I don't know how I'm going to manage any of this. If the Special Service is really here, they won't make a move if they think it'll get us killed. They'll wait for the best opportunity. I keep tugging on my wrists and will the rope to break. Should I wait? Can I?

"Set the play in motion. Make them react to you." That's what Gramps would say on the lacrosse field. You make your own opportunities. The only one who has any power on the field is the one who goes for it.

Now, at this moment, I know in my gut Gramps wasn't only coaching me for lacrosse. He was coaching me for this. My life. He drilled me so hard that, no matter how impossible the situation in front of me, I'd never sit and do nothing. He taught me that the opportunity, the choice, is always mine—if I want it.

We're at the end of the driveway, pulling into the street. I see the baseball cap again, and then I see him, right at the end of the bushes, creeping toward us. For a brief second, our eyes meet. I quickly look away, not wanting Roger to notice. Captain Thompson is here.

I don't see any agents, but that doesn't mean they're not here, too. I tug at the rope around my wrists one more time. Still holding.

It's not the way I want it to happen, but if the Special Service is here, this is the only time. I hope Amber and her mom can get in sync with my game plan.

The strongest weapon I have is my legs. I swing them across the front seat and pull my knees to my chest, just as Roger looks over at me. He snarls an angry string of curses and brandishes his gun. Our eyes lock, and as I scream the most guttural warrior yell I've got back at him, I ram my feet full force against his body, driving him against the car door.

His gun drops to the floor, underneath the steering column, and the Cadillac swerves backward. Simultaneous screeches from the tires and the backseat fill the air, and I'm not sure how fast time is passing, in slow motion or at light speed, but the car crashes hard and I'm knocked forward into the dashboard.

In two moves, Roger hoists me up by my collar with one hand and sweeps underneath the seat for his gun with the other. There's a gurgling noise from the back, and as Roger turns his head, I do the same. Amber has managed to get Lee in a hold, but not the way we planned. Talk about moves. She's twisted around his neck in a wrestling stunt that would make John Cena proud.

Roger yells and bends forward, now frantically searching for his gun. And then it all comes together in front of me like a bad dream. Captain Thompson is slinking down the long driveway, gun drawn. Roger snorts like a bull as he comes up with his gun. He sees the captain and brings his arm across to take aim out the window—he's got a clear shot. I feel my wrists break free of each other and I dig into my pocket for my own gun. I have no choice. I have to shoot Roger. For real. There's no other way to save the captain.

I flip the safety off and am about to pull the trigger when Mrs. Meldon screams, "Clayton, he's got his gun again!" I know

Roger's got a gun, but then I think, *No!* In a flash I shift my gaze to the backseat, where Lee has maneuvered out of Amber's hold and regained control of his gun. It's aimed directly at Amber's chest.

A voice rings in my head. So loud I can't shut my ears to it. *"We serve the people!"*

I know my job. And a rage I've never felt before fills me as I aim at the wrong man's shoulder, knowing Roger is going to hit Captain Thompson, because I must save Amber. Simultaneous blasts echo inside the car as both my gun and Roger's gun fire, and the smoky stench of gunpowder fills my nose. Lee's eyes widen in surprise and he drops his gun and slumps over. Amber struggles to untwist herself from where he's fallen on her, but she and her mom are okay, so I point my gun at the next threat: Roger. Until I deal with him, until he can't shoot anybody else, I can't help the captain, who is lying motionless on the driveway.

Roger faces me with an evil grin, his gun aimed right back at me.

I swallow what feels like hate, what will be hate if the captain dies because he had to come second. "You need to put it down now, before it gets worse for you."

Roger grasps the door handle. "You shoot, I shoot."

I shrug and cock the gun. "If that's the way you want it." I keep my eyes on him and wonder why agents aren't swarming the place. Did Captain Thompson come alone?

A smirk rises at the corner of Roger's mouth. "Kid, who do you think you're playing with?" And then he moves the gun so it's pointing toward the backseat while he opens the door with his other hand.

Crap. Bad guys aren't all stupid.

Now there are sirens, and I hope it's not because a house caught fire. They're getting louder, and Roger starts to step out of the car, his eyes darting back and forth across the road, as if he's not sure which way to look, or go. He keeps his gun pointed at Amber and her mom—I don't dare move, and in a split second

I catch the words tattooed on his neck. The ones I couldn't read earlier.

COLD BLOOD.

I have to stop him.

Roger's eyes are back on me. "I'm leavin', kid. But you cost me big. I might not get my money, but I'll for darn sure get you." I do my best to keep my gun steady as he glares his warning at me.

He turns his eyes once more, this time to the driveway, where Captain Thompson's arm is writhing, grasping blindly for his gun. Roger aims at the captain, and in that instant my blood turns just as cold as his. There won't be another chance to do the right thing. The wrong thing. The only thing.

I pull the trigger—and watch Roger collapse against the car door.

CHAPTER THIRTY-TWO

The sirens are earsplitting now, and I shake myself and check the backseat. Amber and her mom are gaping at me, open-mouthed, but no words are coming out. I get out of the car, open the rear door and offer my hand to help them. They're both unsteady, but Mrs. Meldon seems in better shape than her daughter. That changes the minute Amber's feet reach the asphalt and she shoos me away with her bound hands. "I'm okay," she says, her voice stubborn.

A BMW is speeding toward us from one side of the street, three black sedans on its tail. More sedans and Suburbans than I can count are squealing into stops from the other direction; men and women in dark suits pour out of them, weapons drawn.

"Carlos, over here!" I shout, and sprint to the captain, who lies sprawled on the driveway; his eyes flutter, losing a desperate battle to stay open. At his side, I kneel down and put my cheek to his face and look at his chest. He's barely breathing. I push his dark suit to the side and there it is, all over his chest. It's soaked, a deep crimson color. Why wasn't he wearing a vest?

I let out a moan and inhale the tears back as deeply as I can. Crying won't help him.

I see Amber and her mom talking to some suits, their freed hands pointing first at the house and then at me and the captain. A second later they're all running in our direction.

"It's okay, Clayton, an ambulance is coming," says Mrs. Meldon.

Carlos speaks into his watch and bends over Captain Thompson. "Yeah, ETA seven minutes. Hold on, Captain. Help's on the way."

I look from the captain to Carlos. "He can't wait, he needs to go now," I plead.

Carlos looks at me for a split second, then shouts to the suits dealing with Lee in the backseat of the Cadillac, and Roger, who finally fell to the street. "Brady!" Carlos shouts. "Get those guys away from that car—and if either of them is still breathing, read them their rights." Then he looks at me and the Meldons. "Can you help get Captain Thompson in the back of that car? It's the only thing big enough to had him lying down. We need to make a bridge, and somebody needs to keep pressure on the wound—like this." He rips his chef's jacket off, turns it inside out and puts it over where the captain's bleeding.

"I'll do that," I say.

"Good. Doctors Hospital is less than three minutes away, but you need to get going." Carlos turns to me. "Clayton, I'm going to take care of things here. You go to the hospital with the captain."

I nod. It's not the time to ask questions. In thirty seconds we're in the Cadillac, me and the captain in the backseat, Amber and her mom on the long bench seat in front, with the suit driving like he trained with Carlos in Germany.

I hold Carlos's jacket hard against the captain's chest and pray it's slowing down the bleeding. I can barely breathe as I look at him. Blood is everywhere. Over the captain, the jacket, the backseat and me.

Mrs. Meldon is leaning over the seat, watching us, her face tense with worry. "Keep the pressure on, Clayton, that's the trick. You're doing great."

The Cadillac comes to a shrieking stop in front of the emergency room doors, and in an instant both the suit and Amber crane their necks over the seat, joining Mrs. Meldon. "How is he?" Amber asks.

I shake my head. I have no idea.

Mrs. Meldon flips herself around, opens the car door and runs toward the hospital, Amber and the suit following close behind, all shouting as they sprint through the sliding glass doors. "Somebody help!" "Please! Help!"

I don't take two breaths before they're back, two nurses running after them. One of the nurses opens the car door and sticks her head over the captain and asks, "He's been shot?"

"Yes," I say, removing my hands.

Without looking up, she calls to the other nurse. "Sally! Gurney! *Stat!* Page Dr. Henley! And Sarah! Get Sarah!" Then she puts the jacket back on the wound and presses the same way I had been doing.

In nanoseconds the Cadillac is surrounded by people in various combinations of blue scrubs and white jackets. The next thing I know, Captain Thompson is off my lap and on a stretcher, a team of people barking orders while they push him through the hospital doors, the suit and the Meldons hurrying behind.

And then there's nobody.

I don't think my legs can carry me out of the car yet, so I lean my head back and close my eyes. How did this happen? Why was Captain Thompson alone at the house? What did Laci tell him? Had he come after me, not knowing what was going on?

No matter how it happened, he got shot. And it's my fault.

I think about the doctors who are working on him, and a horrible part of me doesn't want to know what's going on in that building—if they can save him or not. Chills quake down my back and across my shoulders, making every hair bristle all the way down to my fingertips. My body begins to shake and my chest heaves in a fight for each breath. This time, when the tears come, I have no strength to push them back. There are way too many. Tears for my mom and dad, knowing I'll never see them again. Tears for Gramps, wanting his hug. They're all gone from my life. Gone. And now Captain Thompson could be gone, too. And Gran? What about Gran? Where is she?

I drop down and lie on the worn brown leather of the backseat.

Out the window the word *EMERGENCY* glows red across the hospital entrance. *EMERGENCY*.

A buzzing sound comes from the floor of the car and I scoot forward. I look closer and pick it up. It's the captain's cell phone, but it doesn't say who's calling.

I press the green button. "Hello?"

"Clayton! Is that you?" Gran makes a big noise like a sigh and a cry and a groan all put together.

"Yeah, Gran, it's me."

"I'm turning into the hospital parking lot. Please tell me you're here. Please tell me you're okay."

"I'm here, Gran. I'm at the emergency entrance." And then, as I'm about to tell her I'm okay, I lose my voice. The words just stop coming.

The only thing I can do is sit up and step out of the car— and send a weak wave to the black Suburban as it screeches to a stop inches from the Cadillac. The back door pops open and Gran storms out of it and runs toward me. She puts her arms tight around my shoulders and squeezes like she'll never let me go again.

Part of me hopes she doesn't.

CHAPTER THIRTY-THREE

Gran walks me through the emergency room doors and up to the desk. "Someone's told you who I am?" she asks the lady sitting there.

There are suits everywhere, and the woman answers solemnly. "Yes, ma'am, Chief Stone, I'm supposed to escort you upstairs." Then she turns to a man sitting at a computer behind her. "Harold, you take care of everything down here. I'll be back in a minute."

Gran looks at Harold. "Senator Meldon should be here soon—he's very anxious to be reunited with his family. Please bring him to us also."

It feels like an elephant sat on my chest. She doesn't know.

I tug on her sleeve, shaking my head. "Gran, I need to talk to you."

She clutches my arm. "Yes, we'll talk upstairs, Clayton. I want to hear every single detail."

I break from her hold and start to the elevator. We've got to have this conversation ASAP. Then I turn back, and through the glass doors I see a bunch more black Suburbans and a limousine pulling into the parking lot. That can only mean one thing: the senator's here.

I grab Gran's arm and look around. There's only one place we won't be followed by suits.

"Clayton, *what* is the matter?"

"This will only take a minute," I say to Gran. The hospital lady looks nervous, like she doesn't know if she should start escorting us now or stay put and wait. "We'll be right back," I tell her.

And then, as fast as I can, I haul my grandmother into the ladies' room. Thank goodness it's empty.

"Clayton, what are you—"

"Gran, you've got to talk to Mrs. Meldon and her daughter and Ms. Wynn, too. I don't know the whole story, but you were right. They should have questioned the senator. He's behind all of it. The mall muggings and the kidnappings. He had those guys start taking shoppers so when they got Mrs. Meldon and Amber, everybody would think it was part of the crime spree."

Gran raises her eyebrows. "He *wanted* them—kidnapped?"

I nod. "More than that. Amber is his *step*daughter. And he wanted them *both* dead so he'd inherit all Mrs. Meldon's money. I told Carlos, and then I tried to tell Frankie—I guess they never talked to you. Ms. Wynn suspected the whole thing, but I messed everything up. I'm sorry. But you can't let him near his wife or Amber."

She stares at me. I know I sound crazy—I mean, the whole thing *is* crazy.

Without warning, the heavy bathroom door bursts open, and both our heads snap to see Ms. Wynn enter practically in a sprint, and completely out of breath. She comes at me with her arms out. "Oh, thank goodness you're all right, Clayton!" she says, hugging me with one arm while she turns to Gran. "Chief Stone," she says, still puffing and talking fast. "They told me you were in here, and I apologize for the intrusion, but I must tell you something, and I'm afraid it will be hard for you to believe—"

Gran doesn't wait for her to finish. "Are you prepared to give me proof that your boss, Senator Meldon, was behind the kidnapping and attempted murder of his wife and stepdaughter?"

Ms. Wynn's mouth drops open. "Yes," she says.

"Good. That's all I need to know," says Gran. She taps something on her lapel and speaks into it, informing the person on the other end that Ms. Wynn needs *protection* and a ride to headquarters. Then she turns back to Ms. Wynn. "Agent Moxie is waiting for you in the lobby. She will transport you to our offices and take your statement and any other evidence you can offer."

"Thank you," says Ms. Wynn, already moving toward the door.

"No, Ms. Wynn," says Gran with full understanding. "Thank *you*."

As the door closes behind Ms. Wynn, Gran returns her attention to me. "Clayton," she says, the expression in her eyes softening. "You said you're sorry. However, I'm the one who should apologize. I truly thought you would not make a good agent." With a chuckle, she adds, "From what I've seen, though, you have more agent in you than all of us combined."

I go back to the beginning of the week, when Gran and I had our "talk" in the kitchen, and I realize how wrong I was. I could score a hundred goals, or get a thousand As, or help a million people. But nothing could make me feel as proud as I do right now. My grandmother, Chief Stone—the smartest, toughest person in the Special Service, and maybe even the world—thinks I'm a good agent.

Our eyes are locked together, and I'm about to say something like "Thank you" when a rush of noise erupts from outside and, right in front of me, Gran's face turns frozen hard and glassy as a Southern Hemisphere glacier. She makes an abrupt turn, jerks the ladies' room door open and marches over to where three of her agents are standing. Their heads bend together and then she pivots in time to meet the senator as he breezes through the sliding glass doors.

"Senator," she says. "Thank you for coming. You are just the person we need to speak with."

Senator Meldon holds out his hand to Gran. "All the work we've done together in the last two days—it's all been worth it. I will never be able to thank you enough."

Gran ignores his hand and his thanks. "Senator, please accompany my agents—we are interested in learning more about your relationship with the kidnappers."

All movement stops. His staff freezes beside him and the senator pulls back his hand and draws in his chin. "Liza, I'm here to see my family."

"You may refuse, but I wouldn't if I were you." It's clear Gran isn't playing his game. "Rest assured you may see them after we flesh out what has happened this week. The two men who were holding Amber and your wife sustained significant injuries, but I've been informed they are in good enough condition to speak with my agents. And I'm sure you, *also,* want to cooperate fully so we get to the bottom of this. That is the idea, isn't it? To find out who, exactly, put your family in harm's way?"

"Of course," says the senator in a hesitant voice.

"Good," says Gran as she turns to her agents. "Take the senator to headquarters—and be sure to read him his rights. We'll follow when I've got a handle on things here."

"But when will I see Mary Lou—and Amber?"

"Thankfully, they were not harmed, so they may see you whenever they wish to see you," Gran says with a thin smile. "Now, if you'll excuse me, one of my best men was injured while protecting your family. I need to check on him. Come along, Clayton." She gestures to me and moves toward the elevator, where the hospital lady is still standing. "This nice woman has been waiting long enough."

We get into the elevator, and a feeling of relief floods over me as the doors close and I see the senator being led away in handcuffs. He's been caught.

When the elevator doors open on the fifth floor, Mrs. Meldon and Amber are standing there waiting for us. Nobody says anything; we just follow our guide into a hospital waiting room. "Somebody will be in to talk with you shortly," she says before she leaves.

The room is small and simply furnished. A couple of couches and some armchairs and two tables with magazines scattered on top. There's a television anchored to the wall, but it's turned off. None of us is in the mood to turn it on.

We get settled on the couches, and a few minutes later a doctor comes in to tell us Captain Thompson is in surgery.

I can tell Gran is reluctant to ask, but she does anyway. "How bad is it?"

"He lost a lot of blood and went into shock. The bullet struck a major artery, and we're working hard to get him stabilized. We're doing our best, and that's all I can say right now. We've called in the most qualified surgeons in the area, so..."

"How long do you think he'll be in surgery?" Gran asks.

The doctor shakes his head. "Another couple of hours—maybe more. Does he have family?"

Gran shakes her head. "Just us," she says softly.

The doctor leaves, and Gran puts her arm around me. After a while she sighs and says, "Clayton, you're a mess. We've got to get you some clothes. And don't you have a game this afternoon?"

I look down at my bloodstained uniform and then at the clock on the wall. It's a little past noon, but it feels like I've been dropped into a black hole of forever. "Yeah."

"I can have someone take you home. There's enough time."

I shake my head. "I'm not going anywhere." The lacrosse game is important, but this is different. The captain saved my life. If it had been anyone else at that house, he would have waited for backup, or sent agents and stayed in his Suburban like he usually does. Captain Thompson came to get me.

More minutes tick by, and then Amber sits straight up in her seat. "I've got to call Laci—and let her know we're okay."

Gran's eyes spark as though she just remembered some-thing, too. "Mary Lou, I need you and your daughter to give a statement to our agents. The sooner the better, if you don't mind. We won't be able to hold your husband if we don't have cause—and I don't want to give him the chance to pull any strings. He has the means to leave the country fairly quickly, and we certainly don't want that."

She gives me one last hug before standing. "I'm going to send some fresh clothes over, Clayton, but I'll be back as soon as I can." Then she walks to the door and opens it. There are two suits posted outside. She turns back to me and says, "These gen-tlemen will stay with you. I'm also going to visit Masters and let them know you won't be in school for the rest of the day, and I'll try to get hold of your coach." She holds the door open and to the Meldons adds, "Why don't you ladies come with me? I can drop you at headquarters and we can get this unfortunate business behind us."

Mrs. Meldon and Amber get to their feet and come over to the couch where I am. "Thank you, Clayton," says Mrs. Meldon. She sits and puts her arms around me. "We owe you so much." I stare at both of them, not sure what to say. I might have saved them, but I almost made things worse, too. Amber's eyes are tearing up as she looks down at me, and I turn away from her gaze.

"It's okay," I say with a shrug. "I wanted to help."

Mrs. Meldon stands again. "You certainly did that, young man. And you will be thanked properly when all this is over."

I watch them leave: Gran, Mrs. Meldon and Amber. They've got "business" to take care of, and I know I should be okay here, by myself, but when the door closes and the silence returns, this time it's worse. I pick up the remote and turn on the TV, but that doesn't make it any better.

Once my clothes arrive, a nurse takes me to a locker room so I can shower and change. The suits take the clothes I was wear-ing and hand them off to somebody as evidence. A couple of times I wander down the hall and stare at the vending machine, even though I'm not hungry. The suits follow me both times. Mostly, I sit and watch the second hand of the clock go around. And around. And around.

No sign of Gran. I know she has a lot to do. Ms. Wynn. The Meldons. The senator. The school. Coach. I just wish...

And then, finally, a man and a woman, both dressed in blue scrubs with masks dangling around their necks, push through the waiting room door.

They look around, confused, and start to leave.

"Wait," I say.

They both stop. "Are you here for—"

"Derek Thompson," I say, trying to sound as old as you have to be to get information out of doctors.

"Where is your family?" the woman asks.

"They'll be back soon. But please tell me—how is he?"

They both step closer and, looking doubtful, sit in the arm-chairs. The man picks up the remote and turns off the television. "I'm Dr. Clinton. This is Dr. Henley. What's your name?" he says.

"I'm Clayton. Is he okay?"

"Are you Captain Thompson's son?"

I know I can't hesitate, so I don't. But I hope my dad, wherever he is, understands. "Yes."

The doctors exchange glances, and Dr. Clinton gives Dr. Henley a nod.

Dr. Henley clears her throat. "Well, Clayton, we left your father sleeping comfortably. He came through surgery and is doing better than we could have expected. We repaired the artery and did our best with the rest of the damage—he'll need a lot of therapy, but eventually he should have full use of his arm again."

I sink back into the couch.

"Can I see him?"

Dr. Clinton leans forward. "Where is your mother?"

The truth. "She's not here. My grandmother had to go because she works with the Special Service. She's trying to get the people who did this to—my dad."

Both surgeons nod as if they understand.

"We'll send a nurse for you—he should be waking up soon. You'll only be able to sit with him for a few minutes, but by tonight or tomorrow he'll be ready for a longer visit."

I close my eyes as they leave. The room is quiet, but it's the kind of quiet I can take.

He's alive.

CHAPTER THIRTY-FOUR

I follow the nurse into the captain's hospital room, and the twin suits are practically up my business. Gran must have been very specific about their orders.

The nurse looks at me and then at my permanent shadows. "I'll be right outside if you need anything, all right?" she says, pointing through the glass wall.

"Thanks." I move closer to the bed.

The captain doesn't seem as big lying down. And he might need even more blood, 'cause his face looks like the life's been sucked out of it.

"Hey, Captain," I say, my hands gripping the cool metal bars.

His eyelids quiver at the sound of my voice, so I keep talking.

"Everybody's okay. Mrs. Meldon and Amber. Gran is taking care of everything else. So don't worry. Oh, and the doctors say you're going to be fine, too."

His head rocks against the pillow like he's having trouble getting everything in focus. "Clayton?" he says in a raspy voice.

"Yeah, it's me. Don't move, or anything. I'll be right here. If I'm not—I'll be in the waiting room, er, waiting."

He shakes his head. "What time is it?"

I look around and find a clock on the wall. "It's a couple of minutes after four." I turn back to him. There's something I have to say. "Captain, I want to thank you for saving us. I'm sorry I messed it all up."

He struggles like he's trying to get up. "Clayton," he says, falling back to the pillow.

"Stay still, Captain. One of those wires is gonna come out if you don't stop moving around. Do you want to get me in more trouble?"

He lets out an urgent grunt, and his eyes flash brighter than stadium lights. "Your game."

I shake my head. "Don't worry. There's a guy who can take my spot. I was gonna quit, anyway, 'cause I can't help you and be on the team. Like you said, I have to choose the most important thing."

He starts breathing heavy. "You—must—go." One of the machines starts beeping like an out-of-control car alarm. Three nurses run into the room and push me out of the way.

"Are you in pain, Captain Thompson? What's the matter?"

The captain is straining to get up, his arms flailing. "Clayton. Go."

"But I'm late, and Coach will—"

The nurses misunderstand and start shooing me away from the bed. They think he wants me to get out of the room. "Young man, he needs to rest—you can come back in a few hours. Right now we're going to give him something to relax him."

I peer around her and meet the captain's determined eyes. "Okay," I say. "I'll go. But I'll see you tonight, okay?"

He collapses into the bed with a loud sigh and closes his eyes. That's all he wants to hear.

I turn to the suits. "Can you guys take me to my school?"

The men glance at each other and back at me. One of them actually opens his mouth to speak. "Is that where you're going?"

"Yes."

"Then that's where we're going," he says.

I walk out of the captain's hospital room not caring one bit about the suits and my personal space.

It takes about twenty minutes to get to Masters. I'm late for the game and Coach won't let me play, but I have to at least be there for the team. The captain expects it. Gramps would expect it. I take the stone steps three by three, my two agent buddies right with me.

We sprint down the hall toward the locker room, but I feel something as we pass the administration offices. And then I hear it. "Clayton! Is that you?"

I skid to a stop. "Gran? You're still here?"

Gran and Headmistress Templeton dart into the hallway, their faces creased with concern. "There's a slight problem, Clayton." Gran holds up an iPad. "The news stories are starting to come out about the mall nappers, and Laci, and the senator and his family. We just received word that the local stations are leading with the capture this evening, and the questions have only begun. We can count on a big splash over the next week, and because Laci's name has gotten out"—she pauses and stares straight into my eyes, to be sure I'm paying attention—"reporters are likely already here, at the lacrosse game, and will definitely be here tomorrow while school is in session, trying to get interviews."

I begin to put it all together. "And they could figure things out somehow—if they see me."

Gran nods. "Yes. And to add to our problems, someone has been digging, trying to identify a bald lacrosse player. We're not sure why."

"Oh." It's all I can say.

Gran shrugs. "There's no helping that now, but we need to be cautious about exposing you."

She looks back at Headmistress Templeton, who steps closer and puts her hand on my shoulder. "The game's been interrupted— there was distant thunder, and somehow your grandmother managed to manipulate the weather radar to indicate lightning within a mile. That bought us thirty minutes, but we won't be able to string it along more than that. We had hoped our covert operation might give you some extra time—so you could join your teammates for at least part of the game. But this turn of events changes things. Clayton, your grandmother thinks—"

Gran breaks in to speak for herself. "If you put yourself on the field, Clayton, you could be identified—if one reporter wants to know who you are today, there will be twenty tomorrow. So if you do go out there, it will be difficult to use you at the Special Service again—something I have mixed feelings about, as you can probably guess. Also, you are a very important witness in this case, and I think it's prudent to take a look at protective options." She takes a deep breath and turns, avoiding my eyes. "Clayton, I must tell you that it is in this country's best interest to keep your identity a secret, if we possibly can."

Headmistress Templeton squeezes my shoulder. "We've already explained the situation to your coach, and he's going to speak to your teammates. We've come up with a story that should fix everything."

Gran's right, but if the team's in the locker room, I need to see them, to explain the situation myself. "Gran, we can trust them. I *know* we can. Let me explain it to them. At least enough so they know they can trust *me* again. Please?"

Her eyes are back on me, considering. I know it's a lot to ask.

Finally, she nods. "All right, Clayton. I'll agree. After all, your grandfather always said, 'Trust needs to travel both ways.'"

And with my grandmother's blessing, I take off down the hall, a middle school headmistress, two Special Service agents and an undercover grandmother riding my choppy wake.

CHAPTER THIRTY-FIVE

I round the corner to see Coach's grim expression and the slumped shoulder pads surrounding him. It's like we've been defeated already. Crud. It isn't even halftime.

"Okay, guys, before we go back out, there's something else. It's about Clayton."

There are some groans and a couple of swears. And then the voice of my best friend calls out. "I don't care if it's his birthday. Next time I see that loser, I'm gonna—"

Coach freezes when he sees me, and immediately holds up his hand to stop Toby from going any further. Then his eyes move to Gran and the Special Servicemen. "What's going on?"

Every head whips around to face us with wide eyes and curious stares. I notice some jaws dropping at the sight of my backups. The suits *are* a little intimidating. I move to the first empty bench I see, lift my left foot and step onto it. "Coach, I need to talk to you and the guys. It's pretty important."

He gives me a wary look. "Are you sure you should be here, Clayton? I was about to tell the team what's been going on."

Toby's voice is bone-hard and he barely looks at me. "We're losing by three, Clayton—and we're playing short. What is it you want?"

Wow. He's really pissed. I take a breath and let it rip. "I know you guys are mad. I've missed practice and barely made the games and bugged out on almost everything to do with you this week. But I swear on a hundred Bibles, I didn't have a choice. See, I've been helping the Special Service with the mall napper problem and everything sort of spiraled out of control. The whole deal was supposed to stay top secret. I mean, most people don't even know the Special Service exists."

I look at Toby for a long second before continuing. "Then Laci Peters found out, because I helped her and her mom escape from one of the nappers. And I don't want to get into anything more than that, but the thing is, now that we rescued the senator's family, the reporters are going to be hounding everybody at Masters, mostly because of Laci. Except, somebody is also asking questions about a bald lacrosse player, so—"

I'm talking to everybody, but I haven't taken my eyes off Toby. It takes a minute for understanding to rise in his eyes. "Who you are is a secret. A big one. And you're telling *us*?"

"Yeah," I say. "You guys are as much my family as you are my friends. I trust you. My grandmother is trusting you. The Special Service is trusting you. Anyway, the point is, until my hair grows back and this whole thing dies down, I can't play lacrosse, if I want to keep helping the Special Service. And—I do."

The whole room is so quiet I swear I hear sweat dripping. Mine.

Coach is as straight-faced as the suits who've been following me all afternoon, and the guys are looking at me, and each other, with puzzled expressions.

Percy stands up. "So the only thing some reporter knows is that you're bald?"

I turn back to Gran, and she gives me a slight nod.

I look at Percy. "Yeah, as far as we can figure."

Percy and Toby exchange glances, and they begin to grin.

Percy looks back at me. "So if we solve that, you can play?"

I'm not following, and I shake my head. There's no way on earth Gran's going to let—

Gran's voice cuts in. "What do you have in mind, boys?"

Toby steps forward, and for the first time since Laci complimented his goal, his eyes look—hopeful. "Well, they'll be looking for a baldy, right?"

"Yes," says Gran.

He shrugs, and the side of his mouth quirks as he speaks. "It seems pretty simple. We can all shave our heads—give them twenty-five to choose from."

"Yeah, yeah, yeah," Percy says, wagging his head. Excited murmurs grow fast around us.

The entire team is on their feet, clamoring around Coach, and me, pleading. They're a hundred percent in. They want me to play, even more than they want to win.

I face Gran, but she and Headmistress Templeton are deep in discussion.

"I don't know how I'm going to explain it to the parents, but if you're okay with it, I am," says the headmistress.

My heart leaps, and I put my hand on Gran's arm. "I think it'll work, Gran. What do you say?"

She meets my pleading eyes and then pivots in the suits' direction without saying another word to me. "There's a drugstore on the next block. You two have ten minutes to get back here with everything we need, understand?"

"Yes, Chief," they say as they about-face and stride past the lockers and through the double doors at government-issued velocity.

As soon as the suits disappear, Gran says to Coach, "I'm sorry, Coach, I didn't ask if this plan meets with your approval."

Coach glances at his watch and opens his hands in an easygoing gesture. "Exactly seven minutes ago, I got a call from the president of the United States, and that's when I figured out I'm not the boss around here anymore." Coach scans the room and bellows. "We still have some time left in the second quarter. Shall we do this thing at the half?"

And that's when the room explodes.

In a really good way.

Seventeen minutes later, I'm dressed out, and by the time the team piles through the door, we're ready for them. Gran gives Coach a smile and then turns and makes a sweeping gesture toward the mini–makeover operation we've set up.

Half a dozen clippers, razors, shaving cream, towels and buckets of water. It's all there, staggered among the locker room benches—and we've taken our stations. Me, Gran, Headmistress Templeton and the two suits.

Coach nods approvingly. "You've been busy."

I bite my lip, because Coach doesn't know the half of it. Gran claps her hands together and raises her voice above the clamor. "You boys line up, and keep in mind we can get this done faster if you hold still."

It doesn't take long before the entire locker room floor is carpeted in frizzy red curls, long strands of blond, and shags of every shade of brown and black hair. If it's a type or color, our team has it covered—or uncovered.

Toby's my last victim.

I hold up the clippers and admire his first stripe. I'm getting pretty darn good—maybe I can start helping the Special Service with their makeovers. "It's been hard not to tell you. I just couldn't."

Toby grins back at me, shaking his head like it's okay now. Mostly.

"Hey! Stay still, before your head looks like mine," I warn him. "So we're cool?"

"Yeah," he says.

A few seconds of silence pass before I get the guts to spill what's been on my mind. "Listen, I should tell you, Laci's not so bad."

He shakes out the clumps of dark hair covering his jersey. "You don't hate her anymore?" he says, lifting his fingers for a feel of his newly whiskered scalp.

I pick up the shaving cream and turn him around so I can spray the thick foam on his head. "Nah," I say, spreading the lather around.

He hesitates, and I know the question is coming.

"I guess I mean, do you like her?"

I dip the razor into my bucket of water and start to shave, concentrating very hard on his head.

I have to tell him the truth. Maybe not the whole truth.

"Yeah, I like her," I say as I dip the blade again. "But not the way you do."

The breath he's been holding escapes, and his shoulders relax. "Oh, okay," he says, like he gets it.

He doesn't. But that's okay. Toby and I are always there for each other, even if one of us doesn't know it.

I hand him a towel for his cue-ball head and turn to the rest of the locker room. Coach stands next to Gran with his own newly shaved head and blows his whistle twice. "Line up at the door when you're ready to go. And remember, hydrate. We've got a game to win!"

All at once, my feet are like lead and I'm stuck in place. I can't believe it as I watch the guys hustle around the room, passing looks and high-fiving each other like they're in on a big conspiracy. They aren't even thinking about it. Not only is this okay, it's more than okay.

Coach blows the whistle again, and I take a deep breath. Somehow I find my feet and step in with my teammates to get in line. We're ready.

And in a statement to the world, helmets in hand, twenty-five shaved heads march onto the field.

Me and my brothers.

CHAPTER THIRTY-SIX

I open the hospital room door, expecting dim lights and the steady beep of a heart monitor. Instead, it's chaos. At least five suits, my grandmother the chief, and Carlos, dressed in a spotless chef's coat and the tallest white hat I've ever seen, have each staked out territory around the small room. Gran is fussing with her new iPhone—the one with the classified number nobody told me about—while Carlos is poised at the head of the hospital bed, ready to pounce on the captain with a plate of rainbow Jell-O the second he opens his eyes.

On the other side of the bed, a nurse works among the wires, looking from the monitors to Captain Thompson. He's propped upright against the pillow, his mouth open and nostrils flaring, his baritone snores trumpeting above all the other noise.

Nobody notices me until I'm beside the bed, my hands gripping the bars for balance.

"Clayton," says Gran, suddenly next to me. "I didn't tell him about the game. He wanted to hear it from you."

"Really?" I say, with a swift glance toward the nurse. "He's okay? He's been awake?"

I feel a dozen sets of eyes on me, and Carlos steps up and

puts his arm around my shoulders. He starts to speak, but the nurse cuts him off.

"He'll be fine. I came in to check on him. It's going to take a lot of work to get that arm functioning again. But the doctors say in six months Captain Thompson should be almost as good as new."

Six months. Because of me.

Gran clears her throat and holds her hands up. "Everybody out. Clayton is here to see Derek, and we need to set up the room next door, anyway. The hospital has cleared it for our use. Let's go, let's go," she says, shooing everyone out the door.

Carlos bends down to me and whispers, "When was the last time you ate?"

My stomach tightens at the thought of food—no wonder I'm so fuzzy. I haven't eaten since the Dutch baby this morning. I turn to Carlos. "Breakfast."

He makes a clucking noise with his tongue and shakes his head. "I'll be back in a few minutes," he says.

The room is empty now, except for Gran and the captain. Even the nurse has left. Gran's staring at me from across the bed. Her eyes are full and shimmer in the fluorescent light.

There's something I've needed to say for two days. "Gran, I'm sorry I left you when you fell."

"No, Clayton. You did exactly what your grandfather or I would have done. You did what we taught you to do. The right thing. *We serve the people*, remember?" A single tear runs down her cheek, and then she chuckles. "Of course, when you were little your grandfather would say it a little differently."

Huh? "What do you mean?"

"You *don't* remember. Oh, well, I'm sure it will come to you. Besides, I'm the one who's regretful. I've left you again and again—I think everyone has. And today of all days—your birthday." Gran sighs and shakes her head. "But that's going to change—and next year we'll celebrate with a bit less fanfare. I promise."

I don't know what "change" means, and it really doesn't matter. I walk around the bed and into her arms, and something that's been missing is there. She hugs me with the strength and love of eight arms. I'm beginning to feel like maybe I can have a real family again.

After a couple of minutes, Gran rubs my head. "Are you going to let it grow out, or are you and your team going to keep the new look?"

I smile back at her. "Who knows?"

There's a big snort, and we both turn to see the captain's eyes fluttering open. He gurgles something and licks his dry lips as he slowly finds his voice.

"From now on," he says, "Clayton's hair is a matter of national security. Any proposed changes need to go through appropriate channels."

Gran's lips curl in a teasing smile. "Yes, I suppose you're right," she says. She gives me one more squeeze and walks to the door. "I think I'll go see what's going on next door. Clayton can tell you all about the game."

"Hey, Gran," I say, remembering the plans Toby and I made. "Do you think I could go to the gymnastics meet at Crow's tomorrow? With Toby?"

She takes a step back into the room. "I don't see why not."

"And then we wanted to go to his dad's coffee shop for a little while."

There's a look on Gran's face that I seriously don't like.

"Just you and Toby?"

"Er, maybe Laci and Amber, too."

Gran bites her lip. "I'm guessing you don't want me to tag along?"

I start to answer, but she waves her hand. "Of course you can go, Clayton. In fact, take the whole weekend off." And then she walks away and lets the door glide closed behind her.

I turn back to Captain Thompson. He's still pale, but his eyes are completely open, drilling into me.

"What?" I say. "It's something to do."

He shakes his head back and forth against the pillow. "I wasn't going to say anything."

"Gran said you were asking about the game. We won."

"I knew you would," he says. "But I want to talk to you about something else. It's important."

"Okay," I say.

He takes a deep breath and sighs. "I'm alive because of you."

He's giving me credit? He also could have been dead because of me. I move closer and start to argue. "No. If I hadn't—"

He gestures for me to stop, holding up his tube-covered hand. "Clayton, I mean, I'm *alive*. My life has changed, because of you." His gaze shifts and he stares out the window. "Your grandfather was my partner. Since he died, I've—been alone. And until this assignment, until you, I was getting ready to resign from my position at the Special Service. But you've made me remember why we're doing this." His lips tighten for a moment before he continues. "Clayton, you, me, your grandmother—we still have a lot of work to do. And you know how I know?"

"No," I say. But I do know.

"I know because Big Stone, your grandfather, is still here. He's working through you."

We stare at each other, gazes fused together.

"You know, I told them you were my dad."

Is he surprised? Whatever it is, it takes him a second to respond. "Well, you know, that's about right. Because when I lost my dad, Big Stone became my father."

Before we can say another word, the door flies open and Carlos bursts into the room like he's the best float in the Macy's Thanksgiving Day Parade. "I hear it's somebody's birthday!" he hollers as he rolls a silver cart, complete with roses and, of course, candles, across the linoleum floor. His eyes sweep the room, and his grin grows even wider when he sees that the captain's awake. "It's about time you woke up, you lazy slug," he says with a wink in my direction.

He gestures to the cart and looks back at the captain apologetically. "You get my Jell-O surprise, doctor's orders." Then he returns his attention to me. "Clayton, it's not much, but I figure we should mark the day. Sit and eat. And after you're finished, I want to hear all about this monumental game everyone's talking about."

The aroma of the best bacon cheeseburger in town fills the room, and before my butt even hits the chair the first bite is in my mouth and down my throat.

I take a slurp of my Coke to wash it down, and just as I'm swallowing, I notice the twelve-inch pickle decorated with American flags, M&M's and whipped cream set on a pedestal beside my dish of fries. Carlos leans in, lights a sparkler and sticks it in the middle of the pickle. Then he salutes me.

"Thanks, Carlos," I sputter, choking back a laugh.

He shrugs. "I figure you deserve some sort of recognition. We'll have your cake later."

At that exact moment, Gran walks back in, camera in hand, ready to take her annual birthday photo. "Happy birthday, Clayton!" she says as she leans in and points the lens at me. "Quite a plate you've got there." And as I look down at the giant flaming pickle, I remember what Gran wanted me to remember. What Gramps always said.

"We serve the pickles."

And holy mother of undercover! We do.